THE DAYS OF
ABANDONMENT

Elena Ferrante

THE DAYS OF ABANDONMENT

*Translated from the Italian
by Ann Goldstein*

Europa
editions

Europa Editions
116 East 16th Street
12th floor
New York, N.Y. 10003
www.europaeditions.com
info@europaeditions.com

First published in 2002 in Italy by Edizioni e/o

Library of Congress Cataloging in Publication Data is available
ISBN 1-933372-00-1

Ferrante, Elena
The Days of Abandonment

Book design by Emanuele Ragnisco
www.mekkanografici.com

Printed in Italy
Arti Grafiche La Moderna – Rome

THE DAYS OF
ABANDONMENT

1.

One April afternoon, right after lunch, my husband announced that he wanted to leave me. He did it while we were clearing the table; the children were quarreling as usual in the next room, the dog was dreaming, growling beside the radiator. He told me that he was confused, that he was having terrible moments of weariness, of dissatisfaction, perhaps of cowardice. He talked for a long time about our fifteen years of marriage, about the children, and admitted that he had nothing to reproach us with, neither them nor me. He was composed, as always, apart from an extravagant gesture of his right hand when he explained to me, with a childish frown, that soft voices, a sort of whispering, were urging him elsewhere. Then he assumed the blame for everything that was happening and closed the front door carefully behind him, leaving me turned to stone beside the sink.

I spent the night thinking, desolate in the big double bed. No matter how much I examined and reexamined the recent phases of our relationship, I could find no real signs of crisis. I knew him well, I was aware that he was a man of quiet feelings, the house and our family rituals were indispensable to him. We talked about everything, we still liked to hug and kiss each other, sometimes he was so funny he could make me laugh until I cried. It seemed to me impossible that he should truly want to leave. When I recalled that he hadn't taken any of the things that were important to him, and had even neglected to say goodbye to the children, I felt certain that it wasn't serious. He was going through one of those moments that you read about in books, when a character reacts in an unexpectedly extreme way to the normal discontents of living.

After all, it had happened before: the time and the details came to mind as I tossed and turned in the bed. Many years earlier, when we had been together for only six months, he had said, just after a kiss, that he would rather not see me anymore. I was in love with him: as I listened, my veins contracted, my skin froze. I was cold, he was gone, I stood at the stone parapet below Sant'Elmo looking at the faded city, the sea. But five days later he telephoned me in embarrassment, justified himself, said that there had come upon him a sudden absence of sense. The phrase made an impression on me, and I had turned it over and over in my mind.

Long afterward, he had used it again. It was about five years ago, and we were seeing a lot of a colleague of his at the Polytechnic, Gina, an intelligent, cultivated woman from a well-off family, who had been recently widowed and had a fifteen-year-old daughter. We had moved a few months earlier to Turin, and she had found us a beautiful house overlooking the river. On first impact, I didn't like the city, it seemed to me metallic; but I soon discovered how pleasant it was to watch the seasons from the balcony of our house. In the autumn you could see the green of the Valentino grow yellow or red; the leaves, stripped by the wind, sped through the foggy air, and trailed over the gray surface of the Po. In the spring a fresh, sparkling breeze came from the river, animating the new shoots, the branches of the trees.

I had quickly adapted, especially since mother and daughter immediately did everything they could to alleviate any discomfort, helping me get to know the streets, taking me to the best shops. But these kindnesses had an ambiguous source. There was no doubt, in my mind, that Gina was in love with Mario; there was too much flirtatiousness, and sometimes I'd tease him outright, say to him: your fiancée called. He defended himself with a certain satisfaction, and we laughed about it together, but meanwhile our relations with the woman grew closer; not a day passed without her calling. Sometimes she asked him to go with her somewhere, or she would involve her daughter, Carla, who was having trouble with her chemistry assignment, or she was looking for a book that was no longer available.

On the other hand, Gina could behave with impartial generosity; she always had little gifts for me and the children, she loaned me her car, she often gave us the keys to her house near Cherasco, so we could go on the weekend. We accepted with pleasure; it was nice there, even if there was always the risk that mother and daughter would suddenly appear, turning our family routines upside down. But a favor has to be answered by another favor, and the courtesies became a chain that imprisoned us. Mario had gradually taken on the role of guardian for the girl; he went to speak to all her professors, as if standing in for the dead father, and although he was overburdened with work, at a certain point he had even felt obliged to give her chemistry lessons. What to do? For a while I tried to keep the widow at a distance, I liked less and less the way she took my husband's arm or whispered in his ear, laughing. Then one day everything became clear to me. From the kitchen doorway I saw that little Carla, saying goodbye to Mario after one of those lessons, instead of kissing him on the cheek kissed him on the mouth. I immediately understood that it wasn't the mother I had to worry about but the daughter. The girl, perhaps without even realizing it, and who knows for how long, had been assessing the power of her swaying body, her restless eyes, on my husband; and he looked at her as one looks from a gray area at a white wall struck by the sun.

We discussed it, but quietly. I hated raised voices, movements that were too brusque. My own family was full of noisy emotions, always on display, and I—especially during adolescence, even when I was sitting mutely, hands covering my ears, in a corner of our house in Naples, oppressed by the traffic of Via Salvator Rosa—I felt that I was inside a clamorous life and that everything might come apart because of a too piercing sentence, an ungentle movement of the body. So I had learned to speak little and in a thoughtful manner, never to hurry, not to run even for a bus, but rather to draw out as long as possible the time for reaction, filling it with puzzled looks, uncertain smiles. Work had further disciplined me. I had left the city with the intention of never returning, and had spent two years in the complaints department of an airline company, in Rome. After my marriage, I had quit and followed Mario through the world, wherever he was sent by his work as an engineer. New places, new life. And to keep under control the anxieties of change I had, finally, taught myself to wait patiently until every emotion imploded and could come out in a tone of calm, my voice held back in my throat so that I would not make a spectacle of myself.

That self-discipline turned out to be indispensable during our little marital crisis. We spent long sleepless nights confronting one another calmly and in low voices in order to keep the children from hearing, to keep from saying rash words that would open incurable wounds. Mario had been vague, like a patient who is unable to enumerate his symptoms precisely; I never managed to make him say what he felt, what he wanted, what I should expect for myself. Then one afternoon he came home from work with a look of fear, or maybe it wasn't real fear, but only the reflection of the fear that he had read in my

face. The fact is that he had opened his mouth to say something to me and then, in a fraction of a second, had decided to
say something else. I realized it, I seemed almost to see how the
words were transformed in his mouth, but I had quelled my
curiosity to know what words he had renounced. It was
enough to note that that painful period was over, that it had
only been a momentary vertigo. An absence of sense, he
explained, with unusual emphasis, repeating the expression he
had used years before. It had possessed him, taking away the
capacity to see and feel in the usual ways; but now it was over,
the turmoil was gone. The next day, he stopped seeing both
Gina and Carla, ended the chemistry lessons, returned to being
the man he had always been.

These were the few irrelevant incidents of our sentimental
journey, and that night I examined them in every detail. Then
I got out of the bed, exasperated by a sleep that would not
come, and made myself a cup of chamomile tea. Mario was
like that, I said to myself: tranquil for years, without a single
moment of confusion, and then suddenly thrown off by a
nothing. Now, too, something had disturbed him, but I must-
n't worry, I just had to give him time to recover himself. I
stood for a long time at the window that looked onto the dark
park, trying to soothe my aching head against the cold of the
glass. I roused myself only when I heard the sound of a car
parking in the little square of our building. I looked down, it
wasn't my husband. I saw the man who lived on the fourth
floor, a musician named Carrano, coming up the path, his
head bowed, carrying over his shoulders the giant case of I
don't know what instrument. When he disappeared beneath
the trees in the little square, I turned off the light and went
back to bed. It was only a matter of days, then everything
would return to normal.

2.

A WEEK PASSED and my husband not only kept to his decision but reaffirmed it with a sort of merciless rationality.

At first, he came home once a day, always at the same time, around four in the afternoon. He was busy with the two children, chatting with Gianni, playing with Ilaria, and the three of them sometimes went out with Otto, our German shepherd, a dog as good as gold, taking him along the park paths to chase sticks and tennis balls.

I pretended to be occupied in the kitchen, but I waited anxiously for Mario to come and see me, to make his intentions clear, tell me if he had untangled the muddle he had discovered in his head. Sooner or later he arrived, but reluctantly, with an unease that each time became more visible, in opposition to which I presented, according to a strategy that I had devised during my sleepless nights, comfortable scenes of domestic life, understanding tones, an ostentatious sympathy, and even added some light remarks. Mario shook his head, I was too good, he said. I was moved, I embraced him, tried to kiss him. He withdrew. He had come—he was emphatic—only to talk to me; he wanted me to understand what sort of person I had lived with for fifteen years. So he recounted to me cruel memories of childhood, terrible problems of adolescence, nagging disorders of early youth. He wanted only to speak ill of himself, and no response I made to counter this mania for self-denigration could convince him, he wanted me at all costs to see him as he said he was: a good for nothing, incapable of true feelings, mediocre, adrift even in his profession.

I listened to him attentively, I contradicted him calmly, I didn't ask him questions of any kind nor did I dictate ultimatums, I tried only to convince him that he could always count on me. But

I have to admit that, behind that appearance, a wave of anguish and rage was growing that frightened me. One night I remembered a dark figure of my Neapolitan childhood, a large, energetic woman who lived in our building, behind Piazza Mazzini. When she went shopping, she always brought her three children along with her, through the crowded narrow streets. She would return loaded with vegetables, fruit, bread, the three children hanging on to her dress, to the overflowing bags, and she ruled them with a few light, foolish words. If she saw me playing on the stairway of the building, she stopped, put her load down on a step, rummaged in her pockets, and distributed candies to me, to my playmates, to her children. She looked and acted like a woman content with her labors, and she had a good smell, as of new fabric. She was married to a man from the Abruzzi, red-haired, green-eyed, who was a sales representative, and so traveled continuously between Naples and L'Aquila. Now all I remembered of him was that he sweated a lot, had a red face, as if from some skin disease, and sometimes played with the children on the balcony, making colored flags out of tissue paper, and stopping only when the woman called cheerfully: come and eat. Then something went wrong between them. After a lot of shouting that often woke me in the middle of the night, that seemed to be flaking the stone off the building and the street as if it had saw teeth—drawn-out cries and laments that reached the piazza, as far as the palm trees with their long, arching branches, their fronds vibrating in fear—the man left home for love of a woman in Pescara and no one saw him again. Every night, from that moment on, our neighbor wept. I in my bed could hear this noisy weeping, a kind of desperate sobbing that broke through the walls like a battering ram and frightened me. My mother talked about it with her workers, they cut, sewed, and talked, talked, sewed, and cut, while I played under the table with the pins and the chalk, repeating to myself what I heard, words between sorrow and warning, when you don't know how to keep a man you lose everything, female stories of the end of love, what happens when, overflowing with love, you are no longer loved, are left with nothing. The woman lost everything, even her name (perhaps it was Emilia), for everyone she became the "*poverella*," that poor woman, when we spoke of her that was what we called her. The *poverella* was crying, the *poverella* was screaming, the *poverella* was suffering, torn to pieces by the absence of the sweaty red-haired man, and his perfidious green eyes. She rubbed a damp handkerchief between her hands, she told everyone that her husband had abandoned her, had cancelled her out from memory and feeling, and she twisted the handkerchief with whitened knuckles, cursing the man who had fled from her like a gluttonous animal up over the hill of the Vomero. A grief so gaudy began to repel me. I was eight, but I was ashamed for her, she no longer took her children with her, she no longer had that good smell. Now she came down the stairs stiffly, her body withered. She lost the fullness of her bosom, of her hips, of her thighs, she lost her broad jovial face, her bright smile. She became transparent skin over bones, her eyes drowning in violet wells, her hands damp spider webs. Once my mother exclaimed: *poverella*, she's as dry now as a salted anchovy. From then on I watched her every day, following her as she went out of the building without her shopping bag, her eye sockets eyeless, her gait shambling. I wanted to discover her new nature, of a gray-blue fish, grains of salt sparkling on her arms and legs.

Partly because of this memory, I continued to behave toward Mario with an affectionate thoughtfulness. But after a while I didn't know anymore how to refute his exaggerated stories of childhood or adolescent neuroses and torments. In the course of ten days, as his visits to the children also began to decrease, I felt a sharp rancor growing in me, and eventually the suspicion arose that he was lying to me. I thought that as I was calculatedly demonstrating to him all my virtues of a woman in love and therefore ready to sustain him in his obscure crisis, so he was calculatedly trying to disgust me, to push me to say to him: get out, you make me sick, I can't stand you anymore.

The suspicion soon became a certainty. He wanted to help me accept the necessity of our separation; he wanted it to be me who said to him: you're right, it's over. But not even then did I lose my composure. I continued to proceed with circumspection, as I always had before the accidents of life. The only external sign of my agitation was an inclination to disorder and a weakness in my fingers, and, the more the anguish increased, the harder they found it to close solidly around things.

For almost two weeks I didn't ask him the question that had come immediately to the tip of my tongue. Only when I could no longer bear his lies did I decide to put his back to the wall. I prepared a sauce with meatballs that he really liked, I sliced potatoes to roast in the oven with rosemary. But I took no pleasure in cooking, I was indifferent, I cut myself with the can opener, a bottle of wine slipped out of my hand, glass and wine flew everywhere, even on the yellow walls. Right afterward, with a gesture too abrupt with which I intended to grab a rag, I also knocked over the sugar bowl. For a long fraction of a second the sound of sugar raining first on the marble kitchen countertop, then on the wine-stained floor exploded in my ears. It gave me such a sense of weariness that I left everything in a mess and went to sleep, forgetting about the children, about everything, although it was eleven o'clock in the morning. When I awoke, and my new situation as an abandoned wife returned slowly to my mind, I decided that I couldn't take it anymore. I got up in a daze, put the kitchen in order, hurried to pick up the children from school, and waited for him to come by out of love for the children.

He came in the evening, he seemed in a good mood. After

the usual greetings, he disappeared into Gianni and Ilaria's room and stayed with them until they fell asleep. When he reappeared he wanted to slip away, but I forced him to have dinner with me, I held up before him the pot with the sauce I had prepared, the meatballs, the potatoes, and I covered the steaming macaroni with a generous layer of dark-red sauce. I wanted him to see in that plate of pasta everything that, by leaving, he would no longer be able to look at, or touch, or caress, listen to, smell: never again. But I couldn't wait any longer. He hadn't even begun to eat when I asked him:

"Are you in love with another woman?"

He smiled and then denied it without embarrassment, displaying a casual wonder at that inappropriate question. He didn't persuade me. I knew him well, he did this only when he was lying, he was usually uneasy in the face of any sort of direct question. I repeated:

"It's true, isn't it? There's another woman. Who is it, do I know her?"

Then, for the first time since the whole thing had begun, I raised my voice, I cried that I had a right to know, and I said to him:

"You can't leave me here to hope, when in reality you've already decided everything."

He, looking down, nervously gestured to me to lower my voice. Now he was visibly worried, maybe he didn't want the children to wake up. I on the other hand heard in my head all the remonstrances that I had kept at bay, all the words that were already on the line beyond which you can no longer ask yourself what is proper to say and what is not.

"I will not lower my voice," I hissed, "everybody should know what you've done to me."

He stared at the plate, then looked me straight in the face and said:

"Yes, there's another woman."

Then with an incongruous gusto he skewered with his fork a heap of pasta and brought it to his mouth as if to silence himself, to not risk saying more than he had to. But he had finally uttered the essential, he had decided to say it, and now I felt in my breast a protracted pain that was stripping away every feeling. I realized this when I noticed that I had no reaction to what was happening to him.

He had begun to chew in his usual methodical way, but suddenly something cracked in his mouth. He stopped chewing, his fork fell on the plate, he groaned. Now he was spitting what was in his mouth into the palm of his hand, pasta and sauce and blood, it was really blood, red blood.

I looked blankly at his stained mouth, as one looks at a slide projection. Immediately, his eyes wide, he wiped off his hand with the napkin, stuck his fingers in his mouth, and pulled out of his palate a splinter of glass.

He stared at it in horror, then showed it to me, shrieking, beside himself, with a hatred I wouldn't have thought him capable of:

"What's this? Is this what you want to do to me? This?"

He jumped up, overturned the chair, picked it up, slammed it again and again on the floor as if he hoped to make it stick to the tiles definitively. He said that I was an unreasonable woman, incapable of understanding him. Never, ever had I truly understood him, and only his patience, or perhaps his inadequacy, had kept us together for so long. But he had had enough. He shouted that I frightened him, putting glass in his pasta, how could I, I was mad. He slammed the door as he left, without a thought for the sleeping children.

3.

I REMAINED SITTING FOR A WHILE, all I could think was that he had someone else, he was in love with another woman, he had admitted it. Then I got up and began to clear the table. On the tablecloth I saw the splinter of glass, ringed by a halo of blood; I fished around in the sauce with my fingers and pulled out two more fragments of the bottle that had fallen from my hand that morning. I could no longer contain myself and burst into tears. When I calmed down, I threw the sauce in the garbage, then Otto came in, whining at my side. I took the leash and we went out.

The little square was deserted at that hour, the light of the street lamps was imprisoned within the foliage, there were black shadows that brought back childish fears. Usually it was Mario who took the dog out, between eleven and midnight, but since he had left that job, too, had become mine. The children, the dog, shopping, lunch and dinner, money. Everything pointed out to me the practical consequences of abandonment. My husband had removed his thoughts and desires from me and transferred them elsewhere. From now on it would be like this, responsibilities that had belonged to us both would now be mine alone.

I had to react, had to take charge of myself.

Don't give in, I said to myself, don't crash headlong.

If he loves another woman, no matter what you do will be of no use, will slide off him without leaving a trace. Compress pain, eliminate the possibility of the strident gesture, the strident voice. Take note: he has changed his thoughts, changed rooms, run to bury himself in another flesh. Don't act like the *poverella*, don't be consumed by tears. Don't be like the women destroyed in a famous book of your adolescence.

I saw the cover again in every detail. My French teacher had

assigned it when I had told her too impetuously, with ingenu-
ous passion, that I wanted to be a writer. It was 1978, more than
twenty years earlier. "Read this," she had said to me, and diligently I had read it. But when I gave her back the volume, I
made an arrogant statement: these women are stupid. Cultured
women, in comfortable circumstances, they broke like knick-
knacks in the hands of their straying men. They seemed to me
sentimental fools: I wanted to be different, I wanted to write
stories about women with resources, women of invincible
words, not a manual for the abandoned wife with her lost love
at the top of her thoughts. I was young, I had pretensions. I did-
n't like the impenetrable page, like a lowered blind. I liked
light, air between the slats. I wanted to write stories full of
breezes, of filtered rays where dust motes danced. And then I
loved the writers who made you look through every line, to gaze
downward and feel the vertigo of the depths, the blackness of
inferno. I said it breathlessly, all in one gulp, which was something I never did, and my teacher smiled ironically, a little bitterly. She, too, must have lost someone, something. And now,
more than twenty years later, the same thing was happening to
me. I was losing Mario, perhaps I had already lost him. I walked
tensely behind Otto's impatience, I felt the damp breath of the
river, the cold of the asphalt through the soles of my shoes.

I couldn't calm down. Was it possible that Mario should
leave me like this, without warning? It seemed to me incredible
that all of a sudden he had become uninterested in my life, like
a plant watered for years that is abruptly allowed to die of
drought. I couldn't conceive that he had unilaterally decided
that he no longer owed me any attention. Only two years earlier I had told him that I wanted to go back to having a schedule
of my own, work that would get me out of the house for a few
hours. I had found a job in a small publishing company, I was
interested in it, but he had urged me to forget it. Although I told

him that I needed to earn my own money, even a little, even a very little, he had discouraged me, had said: why now, the worst is over, we don't need money, you want to go back to writing, do it. I had listened to him, had quit the job after a few months, and, for the first time, had found a woman to help with the housework. But I was unable to write, I simply wasted time in attempts as pretentious as they were confused. I looked despairingly at the woman who cleaned the apartment, a proud Russian not inclined to submit to criticisms or suggestions. No function, therefore, no writing, few friends of my own, the ambitions of youth losing their grain like a worn-out fabric. I let the maid go, I couldn't bear to have her working hard in my place when I was unable to give myself a time of creative joy, intensely my own. So I returned to taking care of the house, the children, Mario, as if to say to myself that at this point I deserved nothing else. Instead look what I had deserved. My husband had found another woman; the tears rose and I didn't cry. To appear strong, to be strong. I had to make a good showing of myself. Only if I imposed that obligation would I save myself.

I let Otto go free, finally, and sat on a bench trembling with cold. Of that book from my adolescence the few sentences I had memorized at the time came to mind: I am clean I am true I am playing with my cards on the table. No, I said to myself, those were affirmations of derailment. To begin with, I had better remember, always put in the commas. A person who utters such words has already crossed the line, feels the need for self-exaltation and therefore approaches confusion. And also: the women are all wet he with his stiff prick makes them feel who knows what. As a girl I had liked obscene language, it gave me a sense of masculine freedom. Now I knew that obscenity could raise sparks of madness if it came from a mouth as controlled as mine. So I closed my eyes, I held my head in my hands and squeezed my eyelids. Mario's woman. I imagined her ripe, in a toilet, her skirt hiked up, he was on her, working her sweaty cheeks, and sinking his fingers in her ass, the floor slippery with sperm. No, stop. I pulled myself up suddenly, whistled to Otto, a whistle that Mario had taught me. Get rid of those images, that language. Get rid of the women destroyed. While Otto ran here and there, carefully choosing places to urinate, I felt over every inch of my body the scratches of sexual abandonment, the danger of drowning in scorn for myself and nostalgia for him. I got up and went back along the path; I whistled again, and waited for Otto to return.

I don't know how much time passed, I forgot about the dog, forgot where I was. Without realizing it, I slipped into memories of love that I had shared with Mario, and I did it gently, slightly excited, resentful. Shaking me back to myself was the sound of my own voice, I was saying to myself, in a singsong, "I am beautiful, I am beautiful." Then I saw Carrano, the musician who was our neighbor, crossing the street and heading toward the little square, toward the street door.

Hunched, with long legs, his black figure burdened by the instrument, he passed a hundred yards away and I hoped he wouldn't see me. He was one of those timid men who are insecure in their relations with others. If they lose their composure they lose it uncontrollably; if they are nice they are nice to the point of becoming sticky, like honey. With Mario he had often had words, once for a leak from our bathroom that had stained his ceiling, once because Otto annoyed him with his barking. With me, too, his relations were not the best, but for more subtle reasons. When I encountered him I read in his eyes an interest that embarrassed me. Not that he had been vulgar, he was incapable of vulgarity. But women, I think all women agitated him, and so he mistook glances, he mistook gestures, he mistook words, involuntarily bringing desire into the open. He knew it, he was ashamed of it, and perhaps without wanting to, he involved me in his own shame. For this reason I always tried not to have anything to do with him; it disturbed me even to say to him good morning or good evening.

I observed him as he crossed the square, tall, made even taller by the outline of the instrument case, with graying hair, thin, and yet with a heavy step. Suddenly his unhurried gait had a kind of jolt, and he floundered in order not to slip. He stopped, looked at the sole of his right shoe, cursed. Then he became aware of me and said resentfully:

"Did you see, I've ruined my shoe."

There was nothing that proved it was my fault, yet, embarrassed, I immediately asked his pardon and began calling furiously "Otto, Otto," as if the dog would excuse himself directly and relieve me of any guilt. But Otto, of a brownish-yellow color, moved quickly through the patches of light from the street lamps and disappeared into the darkness.

The musician nervously wiped his shoe on the grass at the edge of the path, then examined it with meticulous attention.

"There's no need to apologize, only take your dog somewhere else. People have complained…"

"I'm sorry, my husband is usually careful…"

"Your husband, excuse me, is an ill-mannered…"

"Now you are the ill-mannered one," I retorted, forcefully, "and in any case we're not the only ones who have a dog."

He shook his head, made a broad gesture to signify that he didn't want to argue, and muttered:

"Tell your husband not to exaggerate. I know people who wouldn't hesitate to litter this area with poisoned dog biscuits."

"I'm not going to tell my husband anything," I exclaimed angrily. And I added, incongruously, just to remind myself:

"I don't have a husband anymore."

At that point I left him there in the middle of the path and began running across the grass, in the dark region of bushes and trees, calling Otto at the top of my lungs as if that man were following me and I needed the dog for protection. When I turned, out of breath, I saw that the musician was examining for the last time the soles of his shoes, and then, with his tired walk, he disappeared in the direction of the door.

4.

IN THE FOLLOWING DAYS Mario didn't show up. Although I had imposed on myself a code of behavior and had decided first of all not to telephone the friends we had in common, I couldn't resist and telephoned just the same.

I discovered that no one knew anything about my husband, it seemed that they hadn't seen him for days. So I announced, with rancor, that he had left me for another woman. I thought I would astonish them, but I had the impression that they weren't at all surprised. When I asked, pretending nonchalance, if they knew who his lover was, how old she was, what she did, if he was already living at her house, I got only evasive replies. A colleague of his at the Polytechnic called Farraco tried to console me by saying:

"It's that age. Mario is forty—it happens."

I couldn't bear it, and I hissed treacherously:

"Yes? So did it happen to you, too? Does it happen to all men of your age, without exception? Why are you still living with your wife? Let me talk to Lea, I want to tell her it's happened to you, too!"

I didn't want to react like that. Another rule was not to become hateful. But I couldn't contain myself, I immediately felt a rush of blood that deafened me, burned my eyes. The reasonableness of others and my own desire for tranquility got on my nerves. The breath built up in my throat, ready to vibrate with words of rage. I felt the need to quarrel, and in fact I quarreled first with our male friends, then with their wives or girlfriends, and finally I went on to clash with anyone, male or female, who tried to help me accept what was happening to my life.

Lea, Farraco's wife, especially, tried patiently; she was a woman with an inclination to mediate and look for a way out, so wise, so understanding, that to get angry with her seemed an affront to the small band of well-disposed people. But I couldn't restrain myself, I soon began to distrust even her. I was convinced that immediately after talking to me she hurried to my husband and his lover to tell them in minute detail how I was reacting, how I was managing with the children and the dog, how much longer it would take me to accept the situation. So I abruptly stopped seeing her, and was left without a friend to turn to.

I began to change. In the course of a month I lost the habit of putting on makeup carefully, I went from using a refined language, attentive to the feelings of others, to a sarcastic way of expressing myself, punctuated by coarse laughter. Slowly, in spite of my resistance, I also gave in to obscenity.

Obscenity came to my lips naturally; it seemed to me that it served to communicate to the few acquaintances who still tried coldly to console me that I was not one to be taken in by fine words. As soon as I opened my mouth I felt the wish to mock, smear, defile Mario and his slut. I hated the idea that he knew everything about me while I knew little or nothing of him. I felt like someone who is blind and knows that he is being observed by the very people he would like to spy on in every detail. Is it possible—I wondered with growing resentment—that faithless people like Lea could report everything about me to my husband and I, on the other hand, couldn't even find out what type of woman he had decided to fuck, for whom he had left me, what she had that I didn't? All the fault of spies, I thought, false friends, people who always side with those who enjoy themselves, happy and free, never with the unhappy. I knew it very well. They preferred new, lighthearted couples, who are out and about long into the night, the satisfied faces of those who do nothing but fuck. They kissed, they bit, they licked and sucked, tasting the flavors of the cock, the cunt. Of Mario and his new woman I now imagined only that: how they fucked, and how much. I thought about it night and day and meanwhile, a prisoner of my thoughts, I neglected myself, I didn't comb my hair, or wash. How often did they fuck—I wondered, with unbearable pain—how, where. And so even the very few people who still tried to help me withdrew in the end: it was difficult to put up with me. I found myself alone and frightened by my own desperation.

5.

IN PARALLEL there began to grow inside me a permanent sense of danger. The weight of the two children—the responsibility but also the physical requirements of their lives—became a constant worry. I was afraid I would be unable to take care of them, I even feared harming them, in a moment of weariness or distraction. Not that, before, Mario had done a lot to help me; he was always overloaded with work. But his presence—or, rather, his absence, which, however, could always be changed into presence, if necessary—reassured me. The fact, now, of not knowing where he was anymore, of not having his phone number, of calling his cell phone with restless frequency and discovering that it was always turned off—this making himself untraceable, to the point that even at work his colleagues, perhaps his accomplices, told me that he was ill or that he had taken a leave or was abroad doing research—made me feel like a boxer who no longer remembers how to move and wanders around the ring with his legs buckling and his guard lowered.

I lived in terror of forgetting that I had to pick up Ilaria at school; and if I sent Gianni to buy some essential in a local shop, I was afraid that something would happen to him or, even worse, that in the grip of my preoccupations I would forget his existence and wouldn't remember to make sure that he had returned.

So I was in an unstable condition, to which I reacted with a tense, depleted self-control. My head was completely preoccupied with Mario, with fantasies about him and that woman, with the reexamination of our past, with a mania to understand how I had been inadequate; and at the same time I was desperately vigilant about the obligatory daily tasks; be careful to salt the pasta, be careful not to salt it twice, be careful to note the expiration date of food, be careful not to leave the gas on.

One night I heard a noise in the house, like a piece of paper gliding quickly over the floor, pushed by a current of air.

The dog whined in fear. Otto, although a German shepherd, was not very courageous.

I got up, I looked under the bed, under the dresser. From the dust that had accumulated under the night table, I saw a black shape dart out, leave my room, and enter the children's room as the dog barked.

I ran to their room, turned on the light, pulled them sleeping out of their beds, and closed the door. My fear frightened them, so I slowly found the strength to calm myself down. I told Gianni to get the broom, and he, a child of deep diligence, returned immediately with the dustpan as well. Ilaria on the other hand began to scream:

"I want Daddy, call Daddy."

I stated angrily:

"Your father has left us. He's gone to live in another place with another woman, we're no use to him anymore."

In spite of my horror at any living creature that evokes reptiles, I cautiously opened the door of the children's room, pushed back Otto, who wanted to go in, and closed the door behind me.

I had to start from there, I said to myself. No more softness, I was alone. I stuck the broom with fury and disgust under the children's beds, then under the armoire. A yellowish-green lizard that had somehow gotten up to the fifth floor slid rapidly along the wall looking for a hole, a crack in which to hide. I trapped it in a corner and crushed it, pressing with the weight of my whole body on the broom handle. Afterward, disgusted, I came out with the corpse of the big lizard in the dustpan and said:

"Everything's all right, we don't need Daddy."

Ilaria retorted harshly:

"Daddy wouldn't have killed it, he would have taken it by the tail and carried it out to the park."

Gianni shook his head, came over to me, examined the lizard, and hugged me around the waist. He said:

"The next time I want to be the one to massacre it."

In that extreme word, massacre, I heard all his unhappiness. They were my children, I knew them thoroughly, they were assimilating, without letting it be seen, the news that I had just given them: their father had left, he had chosen, over them, over me, a stranger.

They didn't ask me anything, any explanation. They both went back to bed frightened at the idea that an untold number of other beasts from the park had climbed up to our apartment. They had trouble going back to sleep, and when they woke I saw that they were different, as if they had discovered that there was no longer any safe place in the world. It was the same thing I thought, after all.

6.

AFTER THE EPISODE OF THE LIZARD, the nights, nearly sleepless already, became a torment. Where was I coming from, what was I becoming. Already at eighteen I had considered myself a talented young woman, with high hopes. At twenty I was working. At twenty-two I had married Mario, and we had left Italy, living first in Canada, then in Spain and Greece. At twenty-eight I had had Gianni, and during the months of my pregnancy I had written a long story set in Naples and, the following year, had published it easily. At thirty-one I gave birth to Ilaria. Now, at thirty-eight, I was reduced to nothing, I couldn't even act as I thought I should. No work, no husband, numbed, blunted.

When the children were at school, I lay on the sofa, got up, sat down again, watched TV. But there was no program that could make me forget myself. At night I wandered through the house, and I soon ended up watching the channels where women, above all women, tossed in their beds like wagtails on the branch of a tree. They simpered indecently behind the superimposed telephone numbers, behind captions that promised lavish pleasures. Or they made coy, teasing remarks in sugary voices as they writhed. I looked at them wondering if Mario's whore was like that, the dream or nightmare of a pornographer, and if, during the fifteen years we had spent together, he had secretly longed for this, just this, and I hadn't understood. So I became angry first with myself, then with him, until I started crying, as if the ladies of the television night, continuously, exasperatingly, touching their giant breasts, or licking their own nipples as they wiggled in faked excitement, made a spectacle that could sadden one to tears.

To calm myself I got into the habit of writing until dawn. In the beginning I tried to work on the book that I had been trying to put together for years, but then I gave it up, disgusted. Night after night I wrote letters to Mario, even though I didn't know where to send them. I hoped that sooner or later I would have a way of giving them to him, I liked to think that he would read them. I wrote in the silent house, with only the breathing of the children in the other room, and Otto, who wandered through the house growling anxiously. In those long letters, I forced myself to take a judicious, conversational tone. I told him that I was re-examining our relationship in minute detail and that I needed his help to understand where I had gone wrong. The contradictions in the life of a couple are many—I admitted—and I was working on ours in the hope of untangling and resolving them. The essential, the only real claim I would make on him was that he should listen to me, tell me if he intended to collaborate in my labor of self-analysis. I couldn't bear that he gave no signs of life, he shouldn't deprive me of an encounter that for me was necessary, he owed me attention, at least; where had he found the courage to leave me alone, overwhelmed, examining through a microscope, year by year, our life together? It wasn't important—I wrote, lying—that he should come back to live with me and our children. The urgency I felt was different, the urgency was to understand. Why had he so casually thrown away fifteen years of feelings, emotions, love? He had taken for himself time, time, all the time of my life, only to toss it out with the carelessness of a whim. What an unjust, one-sided decision. To blow away the past as if it were a nasty insect that has landed on your hand. My past, not only his, ended up in the trash. I asked him, I begged him to help me understand whether that time had at least had a solidity, and at what point it had begun to dissolve, and if then it really had been a waste of hours, months, years, or if, instead, a secret meaning redeemed it, made of it an experience that could produce new fruit. It was necessary, urgent, for me to know, I concluded. Only if I knew could I recover and survive, even without him. Like this, in the confusion of life at random, I was wasting away, desiccated, I was as dry as an empty shell on a summer beach.

When the pen had cut into my swollen fingers until they hurt, and my eyes became blinded by too many tears, I would go to the window. I heard the wave of wind colliding with the trees in the park, or the mute darkness of the night, barely illuminated by the street lamps, whose luminous crowns were obscured by the foliage. In those long hours I was the sentinel of grief, keeping watch along with a crowd of dead words.

7.

DURING THE DAY, on the other hand, I was frantic, and became more and more careless. I imposed on myself tasks to accomplish, I rushed from one end of the city to the other on errands that were not at all urgent but which I tackled with the energy of emergency. I wanted my movements to seem purposeful, and instead I scarcely had control over my body; behind that activity I lived like a sleepwalker.

Turin seemed to me a great fortress with iron walls, walls of a frozen gray that the spring sun could not warm. On clear days a cold light spread through the streets that made me sweat with unease. If I walked, I knocked into things or people, and often sat down right on the spot to quiet myself. In the car I had nothing but trouble: I forgot I was driving. The street was replaced by the most vivid memories of the past or by bitter fantasies, and often I dented fenders, or braked at the last moment, but angrily, as if reality were inappropriate and had intervened to destroy a conjured world that was the only one that at that moment counted for me.

In those situations I got out of the car in a fury, I quarreled with whoever was driving the car that I had hit, I screamed insults, if it was a man I said I wondered what could have been going through his mind, foul things certainly, a young lover.

I was really frightened only once, when, distractedly, I had let Ilaria sit next to me. I was driving on Corso Massimo D'Azeglio, and had reached Galileo Ferraris. It was drizzling in spite of the sun, and I don't know what I was thinking, maybe I had turned toward the child to make sure she was wearing her seat belt, maybe not. I know I saw the red signal only at the last second, and the shadow of a lanky man who was crossing the street. The man was looking straight ahead, I thought it was Carrano, our neighbor. Maybe it was, but without the instrument over his shoulders, or lowered head, or gray hair. I stepped on the brake, the car stopped with a long, whining screech a few inches away from him. Ilaria's forehead banged the windshield, a web of luminous cracks spread across the glass, immediately her skin turned purple.

Shouts, cries, I heard the rattle of the tram on my right, its gray-yellow mass approached across the sidewalk, beyond the railing, passed me by. I remained mute, at the wheel, while Ilaria pounded me furiously with her fists and screamed:

"You hurt me, you stupid, you really hurt me!"

Someone was saying something incomprehensible to me, maybe my neighbor, if it was indeed he. I came to myself, answered something offensive. Then I hugged Ilaria, made sure there was no blood, yelled at the insistent horns, repulsed the annoyingly solicitous passersby, a nebula of shadows and sounds. I abandoned the car, took Ilaria in my arms, went in search of some water. I crossed the tram tracks, walked in a daze toward a gray urinal that bore an old stamp saying "Casa del Fascio." Then I changed my mind, what was I doing, I went back. I sat on the bench at the tram stop with Ilaria screaming in my arms, repelling with sharp gestures the shadows and voices that crowded around me. Once I calmed the child, I decided to go to the hospital. I remember that I had only one clear, insistent thought: someone will tell Mario that his daughter is injured and then he will appear.

But Ilaria turned out to be in excellent shape. She merely carried for a long time and with a certain pride a violet bump in the middle of her forehead, nothing for anyone to worry about, least of all her father, if anyone had even told him about it. The only nagging memory of that day remained my own thought, a proof of desperate malice, my instinctive desire to use the child to bring Mario home and say to him: Do you see what can happen if you're not here? Isn't it clear where you're pushing me, day after day?

I was ashamed of myself. Yet I couldn't do anything about it, I couldn't think of anything except how to get him back. I soon developed an obsession to see him, tell him that I could no longer manage, show him how diminished I was without him. I was sure that, stricken by a kind of blindness, he had lost the capacity to place me and the children in our true situation and imagined that we continued to live as we always had, peacefully. Maybe he even thought we were a little relieved, because finally I didn't have to worry about him, and the children didn't have to fear his authority, and so Gianni was no longer reprimanded if he hit Ilaria and Ilaria was no longer reprimanded if she tormented her brother, and we all lived— we on one side, he on the other—happily. It was essential—I said to myself—to open his eyes. I hoped that if he could see us, if he knew about the state of the house, if he could follow for a single day our life as it had become—disorderly, anxious, taut as a wire digging into the flesh—if he could read my letters and understand the serious work I was doing to sort out the breakdowns of our relationship, he would immediately be persuaded to return to his family.

Never, that is, would he have abandoned us if he had known about our condition. The spring itself, which by now was advanced and perhaps to him, wherever he was, seemed a glorious season, for us was only a backdrop for anxiety and exhaustion. Day and night the park seemed to be pushing itself toward our house, as if with branches and leaves it wanted to devour it. Pollen invaded the building, making Otto wild with energy. Ilaria's eyelids were swollen, Gianni had a rash around his nostrils and behind his ears. I myself, feeling weary and obtuse, more and more often fell asleep at ten in the morning and woke barely in time to hurry to pick up the children at school, and so, out of fear that I wouldn't wake up in time from these sudden sleeps, I began to get them used to coming home by themselves.

On the other hand my sleeping during the day, which before alarmed me as a symptom of illness, now pleased me, I waited for it. Sometimes I was wakened by the faraway sound of the bell. It was the children, I don't know how long they had been ringing. Once when I opened the door after a long delay, Gianni said to me:

"I thought you were dead."

8.

IN THE COURSE OF ONE of these sleep-filled mornings I was wakened suddenly as if by the prick of a needle. I thought it was time for the children, I checked the clock, it was early. I realized that what had pierced me was the sound of the cell phone. I answered angrily, in the peevish voice I now used with everyone. But it was Mario, and I immediately changed my tone. He said that he was calling on the cell phone because something was wrong with the regular phone, that he had tried many times and had heard only hissing sounds, distant conversations of strangers. I was moved by the sound of his voice, by its kindness, by his presence in the world somewhere. The first thing I said to him was:

"You mustn't think that I put the glass in the pasta on purpose. It was an accident, I had broken a bottle."

"Forget it," he replied. "I'm the one who reacted badly."

He told me that he had had to leave in a hurry on account of work, he had been in Denmark, a good but tiring trip. He asked if he could come in the evening to see the children, to get some books he needed, and especially his notes.

"Of course," I said. "This is your house."

In a flash, as soon as I hung up, the plan of showing him the precarious state of the apartment, of the children, of me, faded. I cleaned the house from top to bottom, I put it in order. I took a shower, I dried my hair, I washed it again because it hadn't come out satisfactorily. I put on my makeup with care, I wore a light summer dress that he had given me and liked. I attended to my hands and feet, especially my feet, I was ashamed, they seemed rough. I took care of every detail. I even looked at my calendar, counted, and discovered with disappointment that I was about to get my period. I hoped it would be late.

When the children came home from school, they were speechless. Ilaria said:

"It's all clean, even you. How pretty you look."

But the signs of satisfaction ended there. They had grown used to living in disorder and the sudden return of the old order alarmed them. It was a long battle to persuade them to take a shower, to wash as if for a holiday. I said:

"Your father is coming tonight. We have to do everything we can so that he won't go away again."

Ilaria announced as if it were a threat:

"Then I'll tell him about the bump."

"Tell him whatever you like."

Gianni said, with great emotion:

"I'll tell him that since he's been gone my homework has been full of mistakes and I'm doing badly in school."

"Yes," I said approvingly, "tell him everything. Tell him you need him, tell him that he has to choose between you and this new woman he has."

In the evening I washed again and redid my makeup, but I was nervous, I kept yelling from the bathroom at the children who were playing and making a mess. I was more and more apprehensive, I thought: look, I have pimples on my chin and forehead, I've never been lucky in my life.

Then I had the idea of putting on a pair of earrings that had belonged to Mario's grandmother, which were very dear to him; his mother, too, had worn them all her life. They were valuable; in fifteen years he had let me wear them only once, for his brother's wedding, and even then he had been difficult. He was jealous of them not out of fear that I would lose them or that they would be stolen or because he considered them his exclusive property. I think, rather, he was afraid that seeing them on me would spoil some memories or fantasies of child-hood and adolescence.

I decided to show him once and for all that I was the only possible incarnation of those fantasies. I gazed in the mirror and, though I seemed thin, and there were shadows around my eyes, and my complexion had a yellowish tint that blush could-n't hide, I thought I looked beautiful or, to be more exact, I wanted at any cost to appear beautiful. I needed confidence. My skin was still smooth. It didn't show my thirty-eight years. If I could conceal from myself the impression that the life had been drained out of me like blood and saliva and mucus from a patient during an operation, maybe I could deceive Mario as well.

But immediately I felt depressed. My eyelids were heavy, my back ached, I wanted to cry. I looked at my underpants, they were stained with blood. I pronounced an ugly obscenity in my dialect, and with such an angry snap in my voice that I was afraid the children had heard me. I washed again, changed. Finally the doorbell rang.

Right away I was annoyed, the master was acting like a stranger, he wasn't using the keys to his own house, he wanted to underline the fact that he was only visiting. Otto, first of all, hurtled down the hall, leaping madly, sniffing breathlessly, barking enthusiastically in recognition. Then Gianni arrived. He opened the door and turned to stone as if at attention. Then, close to her brother, almost hiding behind him, but smiling, eyes bright, came Ilaria. I stood at the end of the hall, near the kitchen door.

Mario entered loaded with packages. I hadn't seen him for exactly thirty-four days. He seemed younger, better cared for in his appearance, even more rested, and my stomach contracted so painfully that I felt I was about to faint. In his body, in his face, there was no trace of our absence. While I bore— as soon as his startled gaze touched me I was certain of it—all the signs of suffering, he could not hide those of well-being, perhaps of happiness.

"Children, leave your father alone," I said in a falsely cheerful voice, when Ilaria and Gianni had stopped unwrapping the gifts and jumping on his neck and kissing him and fighting to get his attention. But they didn't listen. I stayed in a corner,

vexed, while Ilaria, primping, tried on the dress her father had
brought her, and Gianni sent a remote-control car speeding
down the hall while Otto followed, barking. Time seemed to
be boiling over, flowing in sticky waves out of a pot onto the
flame. I had to tolerate Ilaria telling in dark colors the story of
the bump, and my failings, while Mario kissed her forehead,
assuring her it was nothing, and Gianni exaggerating his
school misadventures and reading aloud a theme that the
teacher hadn't appreciated to the father who praised him and
soothed him. What a pathetic picture. Finally I couldn't take it
any longer. I more or less pushed the children rudely into their
room, closed the door, threatening to punish them if they came
out, and, after a big effort to regain a pleasing voice, an effort
that failed miserably, exclaimed:

"Well. Did you enjoy yourself in Denmark? Did your lover
go with you?"

He shook his head, curled his lip, replied in a low voice:

"If you're going to act like that, I'll take my things and leave
right now."

"I'm just asking how the trip was. Can't I ask?"

"Not in that tone of voice."

"No? What tone of voice is that? What tone should I have?"

"Of a civilized person."

"Were you civil with me?"

"I'm in love."

"I was, too. With you. But you've humiliated me and you
continue to humiliate me."

He lowered his gaze, he seemed sincerely distressed, and
then I was moved, and suddenly I spoke with affection, I could-
n't help it. I told him that I understood his situation, I told him
that I could imagine how confused he was; but I—I murmured
with long, painful pauses—however I tried to find order, to
understand, to wait patiently for the storm to pass, at times I

gave in, at times I couldn't manage it. Then, to offer proof of my good will, I took out of the drawer of the kitchen table the bundle of letters I had written to him and laid them carefully before him.

"See how hard I've worked," I explained. "In there are my reasons and the effort I'm making to understand yours. Read."

"Now?"

"If not, when?"

He unfolded the first sheet with a look of discouragement, scanned a few lines, looked at me.

"I'll read them at home."

"At whose home?"

"Stop it, Olga. Give me time, please, don't think it's easy for me."

"Certainly it's more difficult for me."

"It's not true. I feel like I'm falling. I'm afraid of the hours, the minutes…"

I don't know exactly what he said. If I have to be honest, I think that he mentioned only the fact that, when you live with someone, sleep in the same bed, the body of the other becomes like a clock, "a meter," he said—he used just that expression—"a meter of life, which runs along leaving a wake of anguish." But I had the impression that he wanted to say something else, certainly I understood more than what he actually said, and with an increasing, calculated vulgarity that first he tried to repress and which then silenced him, I hissed:

"You mean that I brought you anguish? You mean that sleeping with me you felt yourself growing old? You measured death by my ass, by how once it was firm and what it is now? Is that what you mean?"

"The children are there…"

"Here, there… and where am I? Where are you putting me? I want to know! If you feel distress, how do you think I feel distress? Read, read my letters! I can't get to the bottom of it! I can't understand what happened to us!"

He looked at the letters with revulsion.

"If you make an obsession of it you'll never understand."

"Oh? And how should I behave in order for it not to become an obsession?"

"You should distract yourself."

I felt an abrupt twisting inside, a mad desire to know if he might at least become jealous, if he still cared about possession of my body, if he could accept the intrusion of someone else.

"Of course I'm distracting myself," I said, assuming a smug tone. "Don't think I'm just waiting around here. I'm writing, I'm trying to understand, tormenting myself. But I'm doing it for myself, for the children, certainly not to please you. Hardly. Have you looked around? Have you seen how well the three of us are doing? And have you seen me?"

I stuck out my chest, I made the earrings swing, presenting to him ironically first one profile, then the other.

"You look well," he said without conviction.

"Well, my ass. I'm extremely well. Ask our neighbor, ask Carrano how I am."

"The performer?"

"The musician."

"Are you seeing him?" he asked indifferently.

I laughed, a kind of sob.

"Yes, let's say I'm seeing him. I'm seeing him exactly the way you're seeing your lover."

"Why him? He's a man I don't like."

"I'm the one who has to screw him, not you."

He brought his hands to his face, rubbed it thoroughly, then murmured:

"Do you do it even in front of the children?"

I smiled.

"Fuck?"

"Speak like that."

I lost control, and began to shout:

"Speak like what? I don't give a shit about prissiness. You wounded me, you are destroying me, and I'm supposed to speak like a good, well-brought-up wife? Fuck you! What words am I supposed to use for what you've done to me, for what you're doing to me? What words should I use for what you're doing with that woman! Let's talk about it! Do you lick her cunt? Do you stick it in her ass? Do you do all the things you never did with me? Tell me! Because I see you! With these eyes I see everything you do together, I see it a hundred thousand times, I see it night and day, eyes open and eyes closed! However, in order not to disturb the gentleman, not to disturb his children, I'm supposed to use clean language, I'm supposed to be refined, I'm supposed to be elegant! Get out of here! Get out, you shit!"

He got up immediately, hurried into his study, put books and notebooks in a bag, stopped for a moment as if bewitched by his computer, took a case with some diskettes, other stuff from the drawers.

I took a breath, ran after him. I had in mind a million recriminations. I wanted to cry: don't touch anything; they are things you worked on while I was there, I was taking care of you, I was doing the shopping, the cooking, it's time that belongs to me in a way, leave everything there. But now I was frightened of the consequences of every word I had uttered, of those that I could utter, I was afraid I had disgusted him, that he would go away for good.

"Mario, I'm sorry, come back, let's talk...Mario! It's just that I'm upset..."

He went to the door, pushing me back, he opened it, he said:

"I have to go. But I'll be back, don't worry. I'll be back for the children."

He was about to go out when he stopped and said:

"Don't wear those earrings anymore. They don't suit you."

Then he disappeared without closing the door.

I pushed the door hard, it was an old door, so loose on its hinges that it hit the jamb and swung back, opening again. So I kicked it furiously until it closed. Then I ran to the balcony while the dog, worried, grumbled beside me. I waited for Mario to appear in the street, I cried desperately:

"Tell me where you live, or at least leave me a phone number! What do I do if I need you, if the children are ill..."

He didn't even raise his head. I shouted at him, beside myself:

"I want to know the name of that whore, you've got to tell me... I want to know if she's pretty, I want to know how old she is..."

Mario got in the car, started the engine. The car disappeared behind the foliage in the middle of the little square, reappeared, disappeared again.

"Mamma," Gianni called.

9.

I TURNED AROUND. The children had opened the door of their room, but they didn't dare to cross the threshold. My appearance could not have been reassuring. From there, in terror, they were spying on me.

Their look was such that I thought that, like certain characters in tales of fantasy, they might see more than it was in reality possible to see. Maybe I had beside me, stiff as a sepulchral statue, the abandoned woman of my childhood memories, the *poverella*. She had come from Naples to Turin to grab me by the hem of my skirt, before I flew down from the fifth floor. She knew that I wanted to pour out on my husband tears of cold sweat and blood, cry to him: stay. I recalled that she, the *poverella*, had done that. One evening, she poisoned herself. My mother said in a low voice to her two workers, the one dark, the other fair: "The *poverella* thought her husband would be sorry and rush to her bedside to be forgiven." But he was far away, prudently, with the other woman whom he now loved. And my mother laughed bitterly at the bitterness of that story and of others she knew, all the same. Women without love lose the light in their eyes, women without love die while they are still alive. She talked like this for hours while she cut out patterns and sewed for the clients who still, in the late sixties, had their clothes made to order. Stories and gossip and sewing: I listened. There, under the table, while I played, I discovered the need to write. The faithless man who fled to Pescara didn't even come when his wife deliberately put herself between life and death, and an ambulance had to be called, to take her to the hospital. Phrases that remained in my mind forever. To deliberately put oneself between life and death, suspended like a tightrope walker. I heard my mother's words and, I don't know why, I imagined that for love of her husband the *poverella* was lying on the edge of a sword, and the blade had cut through her dress, her skin. When I saw that she had returned from the hospital, she seemed to me sadder than before; under her dress she had a dark-red cut. The neighbors avoided her, because they didn't know how to speak to her, what to say.

I roused myself, resentment returned, I wanted to throw myself on Mario with all my weight, pursue him. The next day I decided to start telephoning old friends, to get back in touch.

But the telephone didn't work, Mario had told the truth about that. As soon as I picked up the receiver there was an unbearable hissing, and the sound of distant voices.

I turned to the cell phone. I methodically called all my acquaintances and, in an artificially gentle voice, let them know that I had calmed down, that I was learning to accept the new reality. With those who seemed willing, I asked cautiously about Mario and about his lover, with the air of someone who already knows everything and just wants to talk a little, unburden herself. Most responded in monosyllables, guessing that I was trying deviously to investigate on my own. But some couldn't resist, and warily revealed small details: my husband's lover had a metallic-color Volkswagen; she always wore vulgar red boots; she was a rather pale blonde, of indefinite age. Lea Farraco turned out to be the most willing to chat. She wasn't malicious, to tell the truth, she confined herself to reporting what she knew. Meet them, no, she had never met them. About the woman she was unable to tell me anything. She knew, however, that they lived together. She didn't know the address, but the rumor was that it was in the neighborhood of Largo Brescia, yes, in fact there, Largo Brescia. They had taken refuge far away, in a rather unappealing place, because Mario didn't want to see anyone or be seen, especially by his old friends at the Polytechnic.

I was pressing her to know more, when the phone, which I hadn't charged for I don't know how long, went dead. I searched frantically through the house for the charger, but couldn't find it. The day before, I had tidied every corner of the house for Mario's visit; surely I had stuck it in a safe place that now, though I searched nervously everywhere, I couldn't remember. I had one of my outbursts of rage, Otto began to bark, his barking was intolerable, I hurled the phone at a wall to avoid hurling it at the dog.

The instrument broke in two, the pieces fell to the floor with a sharp crack, the dog attacked them, barking as if they were alive. When I calmed down, I went to the regular telephone, picked up the receiver, and heard again that long hiss, the distant voices. But instead of hanging up, I dialed, almost without thinking, and with a habitual movement of my fingers, Lea's number. The hissing was suddenly cut off, the line returned: mysteries of the telephone.

That second call turned out to be useless. A little time had passed by now, and when my friend answered I found her painfully reticent. Perhaps her husband had reproached her or she herself had regretted helping to complicate an already notoriously complicated situation. She said with affectionate uneasiness that she didn't know anything else. She hadn't seen Mario for a while and about the woman she really didn't know anything, if she was young, if she was old, if she worked. As for where they lived, Largo Brescia was only a general idea: it might be Corso Palermo, Via Teramo, Via Lodi, hard to say, all the streets in that neighborhood had names of cities. And yet it seemed to her rather odd that Mario had ended up there. She advised me to forget about it, time would settle everything.

That didn't stop me, that very evening, from waiting until the children were asleep and, at one or two in the morning, going out in the car to drive around, Largo Brescia, Corso Brescia, Corso Palermo. I proceeded slowly. In that area the city's compactness seemed to me torn, wounded by a broad gash made by the shining tram tracks. Like the implacable base of a piston in motion, the black sky, held back only by a tall, elegant crane, compressed the low buildings and the dim light of the street lamps. White or blue sheets hung across the balconies and, shifted by the breeze, slapped against the gray plates of satellite dishes. I parked, I walked the streets with bitter tenacity. I hoped to meet Mario and his lover. I wished for it. I thought I could surprise them as they got out of her Volkswagen, returning from the movies or a restaurant, happy as he and I had been, at least until the children were born. But there was nothing: empty cars, closed shops, a drunk crouching in a corner. Newly renovated buildings were followed by crumbling structures, animated by foreign voices. I read, in yellow, on the roof tile of a low structure: "Silvano free." He's free, we're free, all of us are free. Disgust at the torments that shackle us, the chains of heavy life. I leaned weakly on the blue-painted wall of a building on Via Alessandria, with letters cut in the stone: "Prince of Naples Nursery." That's where I was, accents of the south cried in my head, cities that were far apart became a single vice, the blue surface of the sea and the white of the Alps. Thirty years ago the *poverella* of Piazza Mazzini had been leaning against a wall, a house wall, as I was now, when her breath failed, out of desperation. I couldn't, like her, give myself the relief of protest, of revenge. Even if Mario and his new woman really were secluded in one of those buildings—in that massive one that looked on a vast courtyard, the legend "Aluminum" over the entrance, the walls studded with balconies, not one without its sheet—they would surely have concealed, behind one of those cloths put up to bar the indiscreet eyes of the neighbors, their happiness at being together, and I could do nothing, nothing, with all my suffering, with all my rage, to tear the screen they were hiding behind and show myself to them and make them unhappy with my unhappiness.

I wandered for a long time through black-violet streets, with the stupid certainty (those certainties without foundation that we call premonitions, the fantastic outlet of our desires) that they were there somewhere, in a doorway, around a corner, behind a window, and perhaps they had even seen me and retreated, like criminals happy with their crimes.

But I got nowhere, I returned home around two, exhausted by disappointment. I parked in the street, I walked up toward the little square, I saw the silhouette of Carrano heading for the door. The instrument case sprouted from his curved shoulders like a stinger.

I had an impulse to call to him, I could no longer bear the solitude, I needed to speak to someone, argue, shout. I hurried to catch up with him, but he had already disappeared behind the door. Even if I had run (and I didn't have the courage, I was afraid that the asphalt would tear, the park, every tree trunk, even the black surface of the river), I wouldn't have reached him before he got on the elevator. Still, I was about to when I saw that there was something on the ground, under the double corolla of a lamppost.

I bent over, it was the plastic case of a driver's license. I opened it, I saw the face of the musician, but much younger: Aldo Carrano; he was born in a town in the south; from the date of birth I saw that he was almost fifty-three, he would be in August. Now I had a plausible excuse to ring his bell.

I put the document in my pocket, got on the elevator, pressed the button for the fourth floor.

The elevator seemed slower than usual, its hum in the absolute silence accelerated the beating of my heart. But when it stopped on the fourth floor I was seized with panic; I didn't hesitate an instant but pressed the button for five.

Home, home immediately. What if the children had waked, if they had looked for me in the empty rooms? I would give Carrano his license the next day. Why knock at the door of a stranger at two in the morning?

A tangle of resentments, the sense of revenge, the need to test the humiliated power of my body were burning up any residue of good sense.

Yes, home.

10.

THE NEXT DAY, with some resistance, Carrano and his license slid into oblivion. The children had just gone to school when I realized that the house had been invaded by ants. It happened every year in this season, as soon as the warmth of summer arrived. In dense multitudes they advanced from the windows, from the balcony, they emerged from under the parquet, hurried to hide again, marched toward the kitchen, the sugar, the bread, the jam. Otto sniffed them, barked, unknowingly dragged them, buried in his coat, into every corner of the house.

I quickly got a rag and washed every room thoroughly. I rubbed lemon peel in the places that seemed to me most at risk. Then I waited, nervously. As soon as the ants reappeared, I took precise note of the places where they gained access to the apartment, the entrances to the innumerable hiding places, the exits, and filled them with talcum powder. When I realized that neither the powder nor the lemon was effective, I decided to move on to an insecticide, although I worried about Otto, who licked anything and everything without distinguishing between what was safe and what was harmful.

I rummaged around in the storage closet and found a can. I read the instructions carefully, shut Otto in the children's room, and sprayed noxious liquid in every corner of the house. I did it uneasily, feeling that the spray can might well be a living extension of my organism, a nebulizer of the gall I felt in my body. Then I waited, trying not to pay attention to Otto's whines as he scratched at the door. I went out onto the balcony in order not to breathe the poisoned air of the house.

The balcony extended over the void like a diving board over a pool. The heat weighed on the motionless trees in the park, hugged the blue surface of the Po, the gray or blue boats of the oarsmen, and the arches of the Princess Isabella bridge. Down below I saw Carrano, who was walking along the path, bent over, evidently in search of his license. I shouted to him:

"Signore! Signor Carrano!"

But I've always had a low voice, I can't yell, the words fall a short distance away like a handful of pebbles thrown by a child. I wanted to tell him that I had his license, but he didn't even turn around. So I stood silently watching him from the fifth floor, thin but broad in the shoulders, his hair gray and thick. I felt an increasing hostility toward him that became more tenacious the more unreasonable I felt it to be. What were his secrets of a man alone, a male obsession with sex, per-haps, the late-life cult of the cock. Certainly he, too, saw no far-ther than his ever-weaker squirt of sperm, was content only when he could verify that he could still get it up, like the dying leaves of a dried-up plant that's given water. Rough with the women's bodies he happened to encounter, hurried, dirty, cer-tainly his only objective was to score points, as in a rifle range, to sink into a red pussy as into a fixed thought surrounded by concentric circles. Better if the patch of hair is young and shiny, ah the virtue of a firm ass. So he thought, such were the thoughts I attributed to him, I was shaken by vivid electric shocks of rage. I came to myself only when, looking down, I realized that the thin figure of Carrano was no longer cutting the path with its dark blade.

I went back inside, the odor of insecticide had faded. I swept away the black remains of dead ants, washed the floors again, vigorously, with concentration, and went to free Otto, who was whining frantically. But I discovered with disgust that now the children's room had been invaded. From the loose squares of the old parquet they emerged in rows, with deter-mined energy, black squads in desperate flight.

I went back to work, what else could I do, but indifferently now, discouraged by a sense of ineluctability: that swarming became more repellent to me the more it seemed a demand for an active and intense life that knows no obstacle but, rather, at every obstruction, unsheathes a stubborn, cruel will to do as it wishes.

After spraying insecticide in that room, too, I put the leash on Otto and let him pull me panting down the stairs, from flight to flight.

11.

THE DOG ADVANCED along the path, irritated by the restraint I imposed, by the pull of the collar. I passed the green stump of a submarine that Gianni liked, went into the tunnel full of obscene graffiti, came out near the pine grove. At that hour the mothers—compact groups of chatting mothers—stayed in the shade of the trees, enclosed in the circle of carriages like settlers encamped in a Western, or they watched the toddlers shouting as they played ball. Most of them didn't like dogs off their leashes. They projected their fears onto the beasts, afraid the dogs would bite the children or foul the playing areas.

Otto was unhappy, he wanted to run and play, but I didn't know what to do about it. I was a bundle of nerves and wanted to avoid any occasion for conflict. Better to hold him back, tugging hard on the leash, than to quarrel.

I went deeper into the pine grove, hoping that there would be no one to cause trouble. The dog was now sniffing the ground agitatedly. I had never paid much attention to him, but I was attached to him. And he loved me, without expecting much. From Mario had come sustenance, play, runs in the park. And now that my husband had vanished, Otto, as a good-natured beast, had adapted to his absence with some melancholy and with yelps of annoyance when I didn't respect the established routines. For example, Mario would certainly have let him off the leash already, just beyond the tunnel, and meanwhile would have accosted the women on the benches to soothe them and reassure them that the dog was well-behaved, friendly to children. I, on the other hand, even in the woods, wanted to be sure that he wouldn't bother anyone, and only then did I let him go. He raced around, this way and that, wild with joy.

I picked up a long, flexible branch and tried it in the air, first idly, then with decision. I liked the whistle, it was a game I had played as a child. Once, I had found a thin branch like that in the courtyard of our building, and I whipped the air, making it cry. It was then that I heard people say that our neighbor, unable to die by poison, had drowned herself near Capo Miseno. The news ran from one window to the next, from floor to floor. My mother immediately called me into the house, she was nervous and often got angry with me for nothing, I had done nothing wrong. Sometimes she gave me the feeling that she didn't like me, as if she recognized in me something of herself that she hated, a secret evil of her own. On that occasion she forbade me to go down again to the courtyard, or to play on the stairs. I stayed in a dark corner of the house dreaming the story of the *poverella's* waterlogged, lifeless body, a silver anchovy to be preserved in salt. And whenever, later, I played at whipping the air to get it to whine, I thought of her, the woman in salt. I heard the voice of her drowning, as she slid through the water all night, as far as Capo Miseno. Now, just thinking about it, I felt like whipping the air of the pinewood harder and harder, like a child, to evoke the spirits, perhaps to chase them away, and the more energy I put into it, the sharper the whistle became. I burst into laughter, alone, seeing myself like that, a thirty-eight-year-old woman in serious trouble who suddenly returns to her childhood game. Yes, I said to myself, we do, we imagine, even as adults, a lot of silly things, out of joy or exhaustion. And I laughed, waving that long thin branch, and felt more and more like laughing.

I stopped only when I heard shouting. A long cry from a young woman, a girl who had appeared unexpectedly at the end of the path. She was big, but not fat, with strong bones beneath her white skin; her features, too, were pronounced, and her hair was very dark. She was gripping the handle of a baby carriage as she cried out, and the wails of an infant echoed hers. Otto meanwhile was barking at her threateningly, frightened himself by the shouts and cries. I ran toward them, I, too, was yelling something at the dog: down, down. But he continued to bark and the woman shouted at me:

"Don't you know you're supposed to keep him on a leash? He's supposed to have a muzzle!"

Ugly bitch. She was the one who needed a leash. I yelled at her, unable to contain myself:

"Don't you have any sense? When you start shouting, you frighten the child, the child cries, and you both frighten the dog, which is why he's barking! Action and reaction, shit, action and reaction! You should put a muzzle on yourself!"

She reacted with equal aggressiveness, growing angry with me, with Otto, who continued to bark. She brought up her husband, she said, threateningly, that he knew what to do, that he would resolve once and for all the outrage of dogs running free in the park, the green spaces were for children, she cried, not for animals. Then she grabbed the infant who was wailing in the stroller and picked him up and hugged him to her breast, murmuring words of reassurance, whether for herself or for him. Finally, wide-eyed, she turned to Otto and hissed:

"Look at him! Listen to him! If my milk dries up, I'll make you pay!"

Maybe it was that mention of milk, I don't know, but I felt a sort of tug in my breast, an abrupt awakening of my hearing, my eyes. Suddenly I saw Otto in all his reality of sharp fangs, pricked-up ears, bristling fur, fierce gaze, every muscle ready to spring, the threatening barks. He was truly a frightening spectacle, he seemed outside of himself, as if he were another dog, of great, unpredictable malice. The bad wolf of the fairy tales. By not lying down quietly as I had ordered, and continuing to bark, complicating the situation, he had—I was convinced—committed an intolerable act of disobedience. I yelled at him:

"That's enough, Otto, stop it!"

When he didn't stop I raised the branch that I had in my hand menacingly, but even then he wouldn't be silent. This enraged me, and I hit him hard. I heard the whistling in the air and saw his look of astonishment when the blow struck his ear. Stupid dog, stupid dog, whom Mario had given as a puppy to Gianni and Ilaria, who had grown up in our house, had become an affectionate creature—but really he was a gift from my husband to himself, who had dreamed of a dog like that since he was a child, not something wished for by Gianni and Ilaria, spoiled dog, dog that always got its own way. Now I was shouting at him, beast, bad dog, and I heard myself clearly, I was lashing and lashing and lashing, as he huddled, yelping, his body hugging the ground, ears low, sad and motionless under that incomprehensible hail of blows.

"What are you doing?" the woman murmured.

When I didn't answer but continued to hit Otto, she hurried away, pushing the carriage with one hand, frightened now not by the dog but by me.

12.

WHEN I BECAME AWARE of her reaction I stopped. I looked at the woman, who was almost running along the path, raising the dust, and then I heard Otto whining unhappily, his head between his paws.

I threw away the whip, crouched down beside him, caressed him for a long time. What had I done to him. I had decomposed, as if exposed to an acid, within the perception of a poor disoriented animal. I had struck the brutal blow of what comes randomly. I had upset the stratified structure of experience, and now everything was a capricious flux. Yes, poor Otto, I murmured, over and over again, yes.

We returned home. I opened the door, went in. But the house didn't feel empty, someone was there.

Otto darted quickly down the hallway, recovering energy and cheerfulness. I ran to the children's room, they were sitting on their beds, their schoolbags on the floor, with a look of perplexity. I checked the time: it had happened—I had forgotten about them.

"What's that bad smell?" asked Gianni, pushing away Otto's greetings.

"Insecticide. We have ants in the house."

Ilaria complained:

"When do we eat?"

I shook my head. Dimly in my mind was a question, and meanwhile I explained aloud to the children that I hadn't gone shopping, I hadn't cooked, I didn't know what to give them to eat, it was the fault of the ants.

Then I gave a start. The question was:

"How did you get into the house?"

Yes, how had they got in? They didn't have keys, I hadn't given them keys, I doubted that they would know how to deal with a lock. And yet there they were in their room, like an apparition. I hugged them with excessive force, embraced them to be sure that it was really them in flesh and blood, that I wasn't talking to figures made of air.

Gianni answered:

"The door was partly open."

I went to the door and examined it. I found no sign of forced entry, but that wasn't surprising, the lock was old and would be easy to open.

"There was no one in the house?" I asked the children, in dismay, and meanwhile I thought: what if the burglars had been surprised by the children and now were hiding somewhere?

I went through the house keeping the children close to me, reassured only by the fact that Otto followed us, dashing around, without showing any sign of alarm. I looked everywhere, no one. Everything was tidy, clean, there was no trace even of the ants.

Ilaria persisted:

"What is there to eat?"

I made a frittata. Gianni and Ilaria devoured it, I nibbled on some bread and cheese. I ate distractedly, distractedly listened to the chatter of the children, what they had done at school, what that friend had said, who had been mean to them.

Meanwhile I thought: burglars root around everywhere, they overturn drawers, if they don't find anything to steal they take revenge by shitting on the sheets, peeing throughout the house. No sign of this in the apartment. And anyway it wasn't a rule. I became lost in a memory of an episode of twenty years earlier, when I was still living at home with my parents. It contradicted all reports about the behavior of robbers. Coming home we had found the door forced open, but the house in perfect order. There was no trace of foul vengeance. Only hours later did we discover that the one thing of value we had was missing: a gold clock that my father had given my mother years earlier.

I left the children in the kitchen and went to see if there was money in the place where I usually put it. There was. But I couldn't find the earrings that had belonged to Mario's grandmother. They weren't in their place, in the chest on the bureau, or in any other place in the house.

13.

I SPENT THE NIGHT and the following days in reflection. I felt occupied on two fronts: I had to keep hold of the reality of the facts while sidelining the flow of mental images and thoughts; and meanwhile try to give myself strength by imagining I was like the salamander, which can pass through fire without feeling pain.

Don't succumb, I goaded myself. Fight. I feared above all my growing incapacity to stick to a thought, to concentrate on a necessary action. The abrupt, uncontrollable twists frightened me. Mario, I wrote, to give myself courage, had not taken away the world, he had taken away only himself. And you are not a woman of thirty years ago. You are of today, take hold of today, don't regress, don't lose yourself, keep a tight grip. Above all, don't give in to distracted or malicious or angry monologues. Eliminate the exclamation points. He's gone, you're still here. You'll no longer enjoy the gleam of his eyes, of his words, but so what? Organize your defenses, preserve your wholeness, don't let yourself break like an ornament, you're not a knickknack, no woman is a knickknack. *La femme rompue, ah, rompue*, the destroyed woman, destroyed, shit. My job, I thought, is to demonstrate that one can remain healthy. Demonstrate it to myself, no one else. If I am exposed to lizards, I will fight the lizards. If I am exposed to ants, I will fight the ants. If I am exposed to thieves, I will fight the thieves. If I am exposed to myself, I will fight myself.

Meanwhile, I wondered: who came into the house, who took the earrings and nothing else. I answered: him. He took the family earrings. He wants me to understand that I am no longer his blood, he has made me a stranger, he has exiled me from himself for good.

But then I changed my mind, that seemed to me too unbearable. I said to myself: wait. Stick with the thieves. Drug addicts, maybe. Spurred by the urgent need of a fix. Possible, probable. And, afraid of exaggerating this fantasy, I stopped writing, I went to the door of the house, I opened it, I closed it without slamming it. Then I grabbed the handle, pulled it hard, and, yes, the door opened, the lock didn't hold, the spring was worn, the bolt went in barely a fraction of an inch. The door appeared closed, and yet you had only to pull and it opened. The apartment, my life and that of my children, it was all open, exposed night and day to anyone.

I quickly came to the conclusion that I had to change the lock. If burglars had entered the house, they could return. And if Mario had entered, furtively, what distinguished him from a thief? He was worse, in fact. Entering his own house secretly. Hunting around in known places, perhaps reading my outbursts, my letters. My heart was bursting with rage. No, he would never cross that threshold again, never, the children would agree with me, you don't speak to a father who sneaks into the house and leaves no trace of himself, not a hello, not a goodbye, not even a how are you.

So, on a wave first of resentment, then of apprehension, I convinced myself that I had to have a new lock on the door. But—the locksmiths I called explained to me—even if locks, with their panels, clamps, plates, latches, and bolts, would

properly lock the house door, they could all, if someone wanted to, be unlocked, forced. They therefore advised me, for my
peace of mind, to have the door reinforced.

I hesitated for a long time, I couldn't spend money light-
heartedly. It was easy to foresee that with Mario's desertion my
economic future would be worse as well. But in the end I
decided to do it, and I began to make the rounds of specialized
shops, comparing prices and service, advantages and disad-
vantages. In the end, after weeks of obsessive investigations
and negotiations, I made a decision, and so one morning two
workers arrived at the house, one in his thirties, the other in his
fifties, both reeking of tobacco.

The children were at school, Otto was lying in a corner
completely indifferent to the two strangers, and I immediately
began to feel uneasy. This irritated me, every change in my normal behavior irritated me. In the past I had always been nice
to anyone who came to the door: workers from the gas company, the electric company, the building administrator, the
plumber, the upholsterer, even door-to-door salesmen and
real-estate agents looking for apartments to sell. I was a trust-
ing woman, sometimes I exchanged a few words with these
strangers, I liked to appear serenely curious about their lives. I
was so sure of myself that I would invite them in and close the
door, sometimes I asked if they wanted something to drink. On
the other hand, my behavior must have been, in general, so
courteous and yet so aloof that it would not occur to any visitor to utter a disrespectful word or attempt some double-
entendre to see how I would react and evaluate my sexual
availability. Those two men, instead, immediately began to
exchange allusive remarks, to snicker, to sing suggestively vulgar songs while they worked, lazily. So I had the suspicion that
in my body, my gestures, my looks there was something that I
no longer had under control. I became agitated. What could

they read in me? That I hadn't slept with a man for almost three months? That I wasn't sucking cocks, that no one was licking my pussy? That I wasn't screwing? Was that why those two men kept speaking to me, laughing, of keys, of keyholes, of locks? I should have armored myself, made myself inscrutable. I became more and more nervous. As they hammered energetically and smoked without asking permission and spread through the house a maddening smell of sweat, I didn't know what to do.

First I retreated to the kitchen, taking Otto with me, closed the door, sat at the table, tried to read the paper. But I was distracted, they made too much noise. So I stopped reading, began to cook. But I wondered why I was behaving like that, why I was hiding in my own house, it made no sense. After a while I returned to the entrance, where the two were busy in the house and on the landing, setting the metal plates on the old door panels.

I brought them some beers and was greeted with ill-contained enthusiasm. The older one in particular started up again with his vulgarly allusive language, maybe he just wanted to be witty, and that was the only form of wit he knew. Almost unconsciously—it was the throat blowing air against the vocal cords—I answered him laughing, with even heavier allusions, and, realizing that I had surprised them both, I didn't wait for them to reply but piled it on, so foul-mouthed that the two looked at one another, perplexed, gave a slight smile, left the beer half drunk, and began to work more quickly.

Soon only a persistent hammering could be heard. Uneasiness returned, and this time it was unbearable. I felt all the shame of standing there as if waiting for further vulgarities that didn't come. There was a long interval of embarrassment, perhaps they asked me to hand them some object, a tool, but with exaggerated courtesy, and not even a smile. After a while I picked up bottles and glasses, and went back to the kitchen. What was happening to me. Was I following, literally, the process of self-degradation, had I surrendered, was I no longer trying to find a new measure of myself?

Eventually the men called me. They had finished. They showed me how the lock worked, they gave me the keys. The older one said that if I had trouble I had only to call, and with large dirty fingers handed me his card. It seemed to me that he was looking at me insistently, but I didn't react. I gave him my attention really only when he slipped the keys into the two keyholes, as bright as suns above the dark panels of the door, and kept insisting on their positions.

"This goes in vertically," he said, "this horizontally."

I looked at him in puzzlement and he added:

"Be careful, you can ruin the mechanism."

With renewed impudence he philosophized:

"Locks become habituated. They have to recognize the hand of their master."

He tried first one key, then the other, and it seemed to me that even he had to force them a little. I asked to try myself. I locked and then unlocked both locks with a firm motion, easily. The younger man said with exaggerated languor:

"The signora has a nice sure hand."

I paid them and they left. I closed the door behind them and leaned against it, feeling the long, living vibrations of the panels until they died away and everything was calm again.

14.

IN THE BEGINNING there were no difficulties with the keys. They slid into the locks, they turned with decisive clicks, I got into the habit of locking myself in when I came home, day or night, I didn't want any more surprises. But soon the door became the least of my worries; I had so many things to take care of, I put reminders everywhere: remember to do this, remember to do that. So I was distracted, and began to get confused: I used the key for the top lock in the bottom and vice versa. I forced, I persisted, I got angry. I arrived loaded with shopping bags, I took out the keys and got them wrong, again and again. Then I forced myself to concentrate. I stopped, I took deep breaths.

Pay attention, I said to myself. And very slowly and carefully I chose the key, carefully chose the lock, held both in my mind until the clicks of the mechanism announced that I had succeeded, it was the correct operation.

But I felt that things were taking a turn for the worse, and I was frightened. Having to stay alert in order to avoid mistakes and confront dangers had exhausted me to the point where sometimes simply the urgency of doing something made me think that I really had done it. The gas, for example, was an old anxiety. I was certain that I had turned off the flame under a pot—remember, remember to turn off the gas!—and yet no, I had cooked the meal, set the table, cleared the table, put the dishes in the dishwasher, and the blue flame had remained discreetly lighted, shining all night like a crown of fire on the metal of the stove, a sign of lunacy; I found it in the morning when I went into the kitchen to make breakfast.

Ah the head: I could no longer trust it. Mario expanded, he cancelled out everything that was not his figure, a boy, a man, as he had grown before my eyes over the years, in my arms, in the warmth of my kisses. I thought only of him, of how it happened that he had stopped loving me, of the necessity that he should give me back that love, he couldn't leave me like this. I made a list for myself of everything he owed me. I had helped him prepare for his university exams, I had gone with him when he didn't have the courage to appear, urging him through the noisy streets of Fuorigrotta, his heart splitting his chest, I could hear it beating, amid the din of students from city and province, his face going pale as I encouraged him along the corridors of the university. I had stayed awake night after night making him repeat the abstruse material of his studies. I had taken away my own time and added it to his to make him more powerful. I had put aside my own aspirations to go along with his. At every crisis of despair I had set aside my own crises to comfort him. I had disappeared into his minutes, into his hours, so that he could concentrate. I had taken care of the house, I had taken care of the meals, I had taken care of the children, I had taken care of all the boring details of everyday life, while he stubbornly climbed the ladder up from our unprivileged beginnings. And now, now he had left me, carrying off, abruptly, all that time, all that energy, all that effort I had given him, to enjoy its fruits with someone else, a stranger who had not lifted a finger to bear him and rear him and make him become what he had become. It seemed to me an action so unjust, a behavior so offensive, that I couldn't believe it, and sometimes I thought his mind had been obscured, he had lost the memory of us, was helpless and at risk, and it seemed to me that I loved him as I had never loved him, with anxiety rather than with passion, and I thought he had a pressing need for me.

But I didn't know where to find him. Lea Farraco eventually denied that she had ever mentioned to me Largo Brescia as the probable place of his new abode, she said I hadn't understood, it wasn't possible, Mario would never live in that neighborhood. This annoyed me, I felt mocked. I quarreled with her again. I heard rumors of my husband: he was again abroad, perhaps traveling with his whore. I couldn't believe it, it seemed impossible that he could so easily have forgotten me and his children, disappearing for months, not giving a damn about Gianni and Ilaria's vacation, placing his own well-being ahead of theirs. What sort of man was he? With what sort of individual had I lived for fifteen years?

It was summer by now, the schools were closed, I didn't know what to do with the children. I dragged them around through the city, in the heat, petulant, willful, ready to blame me for everything, for the heat, for staying in the city, for no beach, no mountains. Ilaria, assuming a look of suffering, repeated, in singsong:

"I don't know what to do."

"That's enough!" I often shouted, at home, on the street. "I said that's enough!" I made a gesture of wanting to slap them, I lifted my arm, I seriously felt like it and restrained myself with an effort.

But they wouldn't calm down. Ilaria wanted to taste all hundred and ten flavors promised by a gelato maker under the portico of Via Cernaia. I tugged at her and she dug in her heels, pulling me toward the entrance of the shop. Suddenly Gianni left me and ran across the street by himself, amid honking horns, followed by my cries of apprehension; he wanted to see, yet again, the monument to Pietro Micca, whose story Mario had told him in every detail. I couldn't contain them in the city that was emptying, and raising hot foggy breezes or oppressive humidity from the hills, the river, the pavement.

Once we quarreled right there, in the gardens in front of the Artillery Museum, under the dirty-green statue of Pietro Micca, with the big sword and the fuse. I knew almost nothing about those murdered heroes, fire, and blood.

"You don't know how to tell a story," the child said to me, "you don't remember anything."

I retorted:

"Then ask your father."

And I began to shout that, if in their opinion I was no good, they should go to him, there was a new mother, beautiful and smart, certainly from Turin, I would bet she knew everything about Pietro Micca and that city of kings and princesses, of haughty people, cold people, metal automatons. I screamed and screamed, out of control. Gianni and Ilaria loved the city, the boy knew its streets and its legends, his father often let him play near the monument at the end of Via Meucci, there was a statue that they both liked: what nonsense, memorials of kings and generals on the streets, Gianni dreamed of being like Ferdinand of Savoy at the battle of Novara, when he jumps down from his dying horse, saber in hand, ready to fight. Ah yes, I wished to wound them, my children, I wished to wound above all the boy, who already had a Piedmontese accent, Mario, too, spoke like a Turinese now, he had eliminated the Neapolitan cadences utterly. Gianni acted like an impudent young bull, I detested it, he was growing up foolish and pre-sumptuous and aggressive, eager to shed his own blood or that of others in some uncivilized conflict, I couldn't bear it any-more.

I left them in the gardens, beside the fountain, and set out quickly along Via Galileo Ferraris, toward the suspended fig-ure of Victor Emmanuel II, a shadow at the end of parallel lines of buildings, high up against a slice of warm cloudy sky. Maybe I really wanted to abandon them forever, forget about them, so that when Mario finally showed up again I could strike my forehead and exclaim: your children? I don't know. I seem to have lost them: the last time I saw them was a month ago, in the gardens of the Cittadella.

After a little I slowed down, turned back. What was hap-pening to me. I was losing touch with those blameless crea-

tures, they were growing distant, as if balanced on a log floating away upon the flow of the current. Get them back, take
hold of them again, hug them close: they were mine. I called:

"Gianni! Ilaria!"

I didn't see them, they were no longer beside the fountain.

Anguish parched my throat as I looked around. I ran
through the gardens as if, by means of rapid, chaotic movements, I could bind together flower beds and trees, keep them
from splintering into a thousand fragments. I stopped in front
of the big sixteenth-century gun from the Turkish artillery, a
powerful bronze cylinder behind the flower bed. Again I
shouted the children's names. They answered me from inside
the cannon. They were lying there, on a piece of cardboard
that had made a bed for some immigrant. The blood rushed
back to my veins, I grabbed them by the feet, yanked them
out.

"It was him," Ilaria said, denouncing her brother, "he said
we should hide here."

I grabbed Gianni by the arm, shook him hard, threatened
him, consumed by rage:

"Don't you know you could catch some disease in there?
You could get sick and die! Look at me, you little fool: do that
again and I'll kill you!"

The child stared at me in disbelief. With the same disbelief
I looked at myself. I saw a woman standing beside a flower garden, a few steps from an old instrument of destruction that
now hosted for the night human beings from distant worlds,
without hope. At that moment I didn't recognize her. I was
frightened because she had taken my heart, which was now
beating in her chest.

15.

DURING THAT PERIOD I also had trouble with the bills. I received letters saying that by such and such date the water or light or gas would be cut off because the bills hadn't been paid. Then I would insist on saying that I had paid, I spent hours searching for the receipts, I wasted a lot of time protesting, arguing, writing, and then giving up in the face of the evidence that I had not in fact paid.

It happened like that with the telephone. Not only were there constant disturbances in the line, as Mario had pointed out to me, but suddenly I couldn't even make a phone call: a voice said to me that I wasn't qualified for that type of service or something like that.

Since I had broken the cell phone, I went to a public phone and called the telephone company to resolve the problem. I was assured that it would be taken care of as soon as possible. But the days passed, the telephone continued silent. I called again, I became furious, my voice trembled with rage. I explained my situation in a voice so aggressive that the employee was silent for a long time, then after consulting the computer told me that telephone service had been suspended because of unpaid bills.

I was enraged, I swore on my children that I had paid, I insulted them all, from the lowest workers to the chief executives, I spoke of Levantine laziness (I said just that), I emphasized the chronic inefficiency, the small and large corruptions of Italy, I shouted: you make me sick. Then I hung up and checked the receipts, and discovered that it really was true, I had forgotten to pay.

I paid, in fact, the next day, but the situation didn't improve. A permanent disturbance of communication, like a breath of storm in the microphone, returned to the line, the signal was

barely perceptible. I went again to the bar downstairs to telephone, I was told that maybe I would have to get a new
instrument. Maybe. I looked at the time, very soon the offices
would be closed. I rushed out, I couldn't contain myself.

I drove through the city, empty in August, in the suffocating
heat. I parked, bumping the fenders of the other cars. I walked
to Via Meucci, threw a spiteful glance at the headquarters of
the telephone company, its grand façade of streaked marble
blocks, took the steps two by two. There was a nice man at the
entrance, who was not inclined to argue. I told him that I wanted to go to an office for complaints, right away, to protest a
lack of service that had been going on for months.

"We haven't had an office open to the public for at least ten
years," he answered.

"And if I want to complain?"

"You do it by telephone."

"And if I want to spit in someone's face?"

He advised me politely to try the office in Via Confienza, a
hundred yards farther on. I ran breathlessly, as if reaching Via
Confienza were a matter of life and death; the last time I had
run like that I was Gianni's age. But I had no way of letting off
steam there, either. I found a glass door, closed and locked. I
shook it hard, although it had written on it: "This door is
alarmed." Alarmed, yes, that ridiculous expression, let the
alarm sound, let the city be alarmed, the world. From a small
window in the wall to my left a man stuck his head out; he was
not disposed to chat, and he got rid of me with a few words
and disappeared again: there were no offices, let alone open to
the public; everything was reduced to aseptic voice, computer
screen, e-mail, bank operations; if a person—he said to me
coldly—has anger to vent, sorry, there's no one here to tangle
with.

Frustration gave me a stomachache, I went back along the

street, I felt as if I were about to lose my breath and sink to the ground. As if it were prehensile, my eye grasped the letters of a plaque on the building opposite. Words so that I wouldn't fall. From this house entered into life like the shadow of a dream a poet named Guido Gozzano, who from the sadness of nothingness—why is nothingness sad, what's sad about noth-ingness—reached God. Words with a claim of art for the art of linking words. I went on with my head lowered, I was afraid I was talking to myself, a man was staring at me, I walked faster. I no longer remembered where I had left the car, it wasn't important to remember.

I wandered at random, past the Alfieri theatre, ending up in Via Pietro Micca. I looked around disoriented, certainly the car wasn't there. But in front of a shop window, the window of a jewelry store, I saw Mario and his new woman.

I don't know if I recognized her right away. All I felt was a fist in the middle of my chest. Maybe I realized first that she was very young, so young that Mario seemed an old man beside her. Or maybe I noticed on her, above all, the blue dress of a light material, in a style out of fashion, the sort of dress that can be bought in stores for expensive second-hand clothes, a style at odds with her youth but soft on her body that was rich in gentle curves, the curve of her long neck, of her breasts, her hips, her ankles. Or maybe what struck me was the blond hair gathered at the nape, rolled and held in place by a comb, a hypnotic stain.

I don't know exactly.

Certainly I had to make swift eraser strokes over the round-ed features of the twenty-year-old before retrieving the sharp, angular, still childish face of Carla, the adolescent who had been at the center of our marital crisis years earlier. And, cer-tainly, only when I had recognized her was I struck by the ear-rings, the earrings of Mario's grandmother, my earrings.

They hung from her lobes, elegantly setting off her neck, they made her smile even brighter; while my husband, in front of the window, encircled her waist with the proprietary joy of the gesture, while she rested a bare arm on his shoulder.

Time expanded. I crossed the street with long, determined strides, I felt no desire to cry or scream or ask for explanations, only a black mania for destruction.

Now I knew that he had deceived me for almost five years.

For almost five years he had secretly enjoyed that body, had cultivated that passion, had transformed it into love, had slept patiently with me abandoning himself to the memory of her, had waited until she became of age, more than of age, to tell me that he was taking her definitively, that he was leaving me. Vile, cowardly man. To the point of being unable to tell me what had really happened to him. He had added family fiction to marital fiction to sexual fiction to give his cowardice time, to get it under control, to find, slowly, the strength to leave me.

I came up behind them. I struck him like a battering ram with all my weight, I shoved him against the glass, he hit it with his face. Perhaps Carla cried out, but I saw only her open mouth, a black hole in the enclosure of her even, white teeth. Meanwhile I grabbed Mario, who was turning around with frightened eyes, his nose bleeding, and he looked at me full of terror and astonishment at once. Hold the commas, hold the periods. It's not easy to go from the happy serenity of a romantic stroll to the chaos, to the incoherence of the world. Poor man, poor man. I grabbed him by the shirt and yanked him so violently that I tore it off the right shoulder, found it in my hands. He stood bare-chested, he wasn't wearing an under-shirt, he no longer worried about catching cold, about pneumonia, with me he had been consumed by hypochondria. His health had evidently been revitalized, he had a good tan, he was thinner, only a little ridiculous now, because one arm was covered by a whole, nicely ironed sleeve, with part of the shoulder still attached, and the collar, too, at an angle; while otherwise his torso was bare, shreds of the shirt hung from his pants, blood dripped amid the grizzled hairs of his chest.

I hit him again and again, he fell down on the sidewalk. I kicked him, one two three times, but—I don't know why—he didn't defend himself, his movements were awkward, with his arms he sheltered his face instead of his ribs, maybe it was shame, hard to say.

When I had had enough I turned toward Carla, who was still open-mouthed. She retreated, I advanced. I tried to grab her and she evaded me. I had no intention of hitting her, she was a stranger, toward her I felt almost calm. I was angry only at Mario, who had given her those earrings, so I hit the air violently, trying to grab them. I wanted to rip them from her lobes, tear the flesh, deny her the role of heir of my husband's forebears. What did she have to do with it, the dirty whore, what did she have to do with that line of descent. She was flaunting herself like an impudent whore with my things, which would later become the things of my daughter. She opened her thighs, she bathed his prick, and imagined that thus she had baptized him, I baptize you with the holy water of the cunt, I immerse your cock in the moist flesh and I rename it, I call it mine and born to a new life. The bitch. So she thought she had full rights to take my place, to play my part, the fucking whore. Give me those earrings, give me those earrings. I wanted to rip them off her, together with the ear, I wanted to drag along her beautiful face with the eyes the nose the lips the scalp the blond hair, I wanted to drag them with me as if with a hook I'd snagged her garment of flesh, the sacks of her breasts, the belly that wrapped the bowels and spilled out through the asshole, through the deep crack crowned with gold. And leave to her only that which in reality she was, an ugly skull stained with living blood, a skeleton that had just been skinned. Because what is the face, what, finally, is the skin over the flesh, a cover, a disguise, rouge for the insupportable horror of our living nature. And he had fallen for it, he had been caught. For that face, for that soft garment he had sneaked into my house. He had stolen my earrings for love of that carnival mask. I wanted to rip it all off of her, yes, pull it off with the earrings. Meanwhile I was screaming at Mario:

"Just look, I'll show you what she really is!"

But he stopped me. No passerby intervened, only a few of the curious—it seems to me—slowed down to look, with amusement. I remember it because for them, for the curious, I uttered fragments of sentences like captions, I wanted it understood what I was doing, what were the motivations of my fury. And it seemed to me that those who stayed to watch wanted to see if I would really do what I was threatening to do. A woman can easily kill on the street, in the middle of a crowd, she can do it more easily than a man. Her violence seems a game, a parody, an improper and slightly ridiculous use of the male intent to do harm. Only because Mario grabbed me by the shoulders did I not rip the earrings from Carla's earlobes.

He grabbed me and pushed me away as if I were a thing. He had never treated me with such hatred. He threatened me, he was all stained with blood, distraught. But now his image appeared to be that of someone speaking on a television in a shop window. Rather than dangerous, I felt that it was sordid. From that place, from who can say what distance, the distance, perhaps, that separates the false from the true, he pointed at me a malevolent index finger, fixed at the extremity of his single remaining shirtsleeve. I didn't hear what he said, but I felt like laughing at his artificial imperiousness. The laugh took away every desire to attack, drained me. I let him carry off his woman, with the earrings that hung from her ears. For what could I do, I had lost everything, all of myself, all, irre-mediably.

16.

WHEN THE CHILDREN came home (I had left them with friends), I said that I didn't feel like cooking; I hadn't prepared anything, they should fend for themselves. Maybe because of my appearance, or what they heard in my weary tone of voice, they went into the kitchen without protesting. When they reappeared, they stood in silence, almost embarrassed, in a corner of the living room. After a while Ilaria came and laid her hands on my temples and asked:

"Do you have a headache?"

I said no, I said I didn't want to be bothered. They retreat-ed into their room, offended by my behavior, embittered by my rejection of their affection. At some point I realized that it was dark, I remembered them, I went to see what they were doing. They were asleep, clothed, on the same bed, one beside the other. I left them like that and closed the door.

React. I began to tidy up. When I had finished I began again, a kind of roundup of everything that didn't appear to be in order. Lucidity, determination, hold on to life. In the bathroom I found the usual mess in the medicine chest. I sat on the floor and began to separate the medicines that had expired from the ones that were still good. When all the unus-able drugs had gone into the wastebasket and the medicine chest was in order, I took two packages of sleeping pills and brought them to the living room. I put them on the table, filled a glass to the brim with cognac. With the glass in one hand and in the palm of the other a handful of pills, I went to the window, from which came the damp warm breath of the river, of the trees.

Everything was so random. As a girl, I had fallen in love with Mario, but I could have fallen in love with anyone: a body to which we end up attributing who knows what meanings. A long passage of life together, and you think he's the only man you can be happy with, you credit him with countless critical virtues, and instead he's just a reed that emits sounds of falsehood, you don't know who he really is, he doesn't know himself. We are occasions. We consummate life and lose it because in some long-ago time someone, in the desire to unload his cock inside us, was nice, chose us among women. We take for some sort of kindness addressed to us alone the banal desire for sex. We love his desire to fuck, we are so dazzled by it we think it's the desire to fuck only us, us alone. Oh yes, he who is so special and who has recognized us as special. We give it a name, that desire of the cock, we personalize it, we call it my love. To hell with all that, that dazzlement, that unfounded titillation. Once he fucked me, now he fucks someone else, what claim do I have? Time passes, one goes, another arrives. I was about to swallow some pills, I wanted to sleep lying in the darkest depths of myself.

At that moment, however, from the mass of trees in the little square the violet shadow of Carrano emerged, the instrument case over his shoulder. With an uncertain and unhurried step the musician crossed the whole area, empty of cars—the heat had definitively emptied the city—and disappeared under the hulk of the building. After a while I heard the jerk of the elevator gears, its hum. I suddenly remembered that I still had the man's license. Otto growled in his sleep.

I went to the kitchen, threw the pills and the cognac into the sink, hunted for Carrano's license. I found it on the telephone table, almost hidden by the phone. I turned it over in my hands, I looked at the photograph. His hair was still black, the deep creases that marked his face between the nose and the corners of his mouth had not yet appeared. I looked at the date of birth, tried to remember what day it was, and realized that it was the start of his fifty-third birthday.

I was torn. I felt like going down the stairs, knocking on his door, using the license to enter his house at this late hour; but I was also frightened, frightened by the unknown, by the night, by the silence of the whole building, by the damp and suffocating smells that rose from the park, by the cries of nocturnal birds.

I had the idea of telephoning him, I didn't want to change my mind, I wanted rather to be encouraged. I looked for his number in the book, I found it. I pretended in my mind a cordial conversation: I found your license just this morning, on Viale dei Marinai; I could come down and give it to you, if it's not too late; and I have to confess that my eye fell on your date of birth; I wanted to wish you happy birthday, happy birthday with all my heart, Signor Carrano, happy birthday, really, it's just past midnight, I bet I'm the first to congratulate you.

Ridiculous. I had never been able to use a flirtatious tone with men. Kind, cordial, but without the warmth, the coy expressions of sexual availability. I tormented myself throughout adolescence. But I'm almost forty now, I said to myself, I must have learned something. I picked up the receiver with my heart thumping, and put it down angrily. There was that stormy hissing, no line. I picked it up again, tried to dial the number. The hissing was still there.

I felt the slab of my eyelids lower, there was no hope, the heat of the solitary night would massacre my heart. Then I saw my husband. Now he was no longer holding in his arms an unknown woman. I knew the pretty face, the earrings in the earlobes, the name Carla, the body of youthful shame.

They were both naked at that moment, they were fucking without any hurry, they meant to make love all night as certainly they had made love in recent years unbeknownst to me, every spasm of my suffering coincided with a spasm of their pleasure.

I decided, enough pain. To the lips of their nocturnal happiness I would attach those of my revenge. I was not the woman who breaks into pieces under the blows of abandonment and absence, who goes mad, who dies. Only a few fragments had splintered off, for the rest I was well. I was whole, whole I would remain. To those who hurt me, I react giving back in kind. I am the queen of spades, I am the wasp that stings, I am the dark serpent. I am the invulnerable animal who passes through fire and is not burned.

17.

I CHOSE A BOTTLE OF WINE, put the house keys in my pocket, and, without even combing my hair, went down to the floor below.

I rang decisively, twice, two long electric rings, at Carrano's door. There was only silence, anxiety pounded in my throat. Then I heard slow steps, again everything was quiet, Carrano was looking at me through the peephole. The key turned in the lock, he was a man who feared the night, locked himself in like a woman alone. I thought of running home, before the door opened.

He appeared before me in his bathrobe, his ankles thin and bare, on his feet slippers with the name of a hotel, he must have purloined them, along with the soap, during a trip with the orchestra.

"Happy birthday," I said in a rush, without smiling. "I wanted to wish you a happy birthday."

In one hand I held out the bottle of wine, in the other the license.

"I found it this morning at the end of the street."

He looked at me in confusion.

"Not the bottle," I explained, "the license."

Only then did he seem to understand, and he said to me in puzzlement:

"Thank you, I didn't expect to find it. Will you come in?"

"Maybe it's too late," I murmured, again seized by panic.

He answered with a small, embarrassed smile:

"It's late, yes, but... please, it would be a pleasure... and thank you... the house is a little untidy... come in."

I liked that tone. It was the tone of a timid man who tries to appear worldly, but without conviction. I went in, closed the door behind me.

From that moment, miraculously, I began to feel at my ease. In the living room I saw the big instrument case leaning in a corner and it seemed to me a known presence, like that of a maidservant of fifty years ago, one of those large village women who in cities bring up the children of the well off. The house certainly was a mess (a newspaper on the floor, old cigarette butts of some visitor in the ashtray, a dirty milk glass on the table) but it was the pleasant disorder of a man alone, and then the air smelled of soap, you could still smell the clean steam of the shower.

"Excuse my outfit, but I had just..."

"Of course."

"I'll get some glasses, I have some olives, crackers..."

"Really, I just wanted to drink to your health."

And to mine. And to the sorrow, the sorrow of love and sex that I hoped would come soon to Mario and Carla. I had to get used to saying that, the permanently linked names of a new couple. Before, people said Mario and Olga, now they say Mario and Carla. He ought to feel a terrible pain in his prick, disfigurement of syphilis, a rot throughout his body, the stink of betrayal.

Carrano returned with glasses. He uncorked the bottle, waited a little, poured the wine, and meanwhile said nice things in a gentle voice: I had lovely children, he had often watched me from the windows when I was with them, I knew how to treat them. He didn't mention the dog, he didn't mention my husband, I felt that he found both unbearable, but that in that circumstance, out of politeness, it didn't seem nice to say so.

After the first glass I said so to him. Otto was a good dog, but frankly I would never have had a dog in the house, a big dog suffers in an apartment. It was my husband who had insisted, he had taken responsibility for the animal, and, indeed, many other responsibilities. But in the end he had shown himself to be a contemptible man, incapable of keeping faith with the commitments he had made. We don't know anything about people, even those with whom we share everything.

"I know just as much about my husband as I know about you, there's no difference," I exclaimed. The soul is an inconstant wind, Signor Carrano, a vibration of the vocal chords, for pretending to be someone, something. Mario went off—I told him—with a girl of twenty. He had betrayed me with her for five years, in secret, a duplicitous man, two-faced, with two separate streams of words. And now he has disappeared, leaving all the worries to me: his children to take care of, the house to maintain, and the dog, stupid Otto. I was overwhelmed. By the responsibilities alone, nothing else. It didn't matter about him. The responsibilities that we had shared were all mine now, even the responsibility of having been unable to keep our relationship alive—alive, keep alive: a cliché; why should I be working to keep it alive; I was tired of clichés—and also the responsibility of understanding where we had gone wrong. Because I was forced to do that torturous work of analysis for Mario, too, he didn't want to get to the bottom, he didn't want to adjust or renew. He was as if blinded by the blonde, but I had given myself the task of analyzing, point by point, our fifteen years together, I was doing it, I worked at night. I wanted to be ready to re-establish everything, as soon as he became reasonable. If that ever happened.

Carrano sat beside me on the sofa, he covered his ankles as much as he could with the dressing gown, he sipped his wine listening attentively to what I was saying. He never interrupted, but managed to communicate to me such a certainty of listening that I felt not a single word, not an emotion, was wasted, and I wasn't ashamed when I felt like crying. I burst out crying without hesitation, sure that he understood me, and I felt something move inside me, a jolt of grief so intense that the tears seemed to me fragments of a crystal object stored for a long time in a secret place and now, because of that movement, shattered into a thousand stabbing shards. My eyes felt wounded, and my nose, yet I couldn't stop. And I was moved even more when I realized that Carrano, too, could not contain himself, his lower lip was trembling, his eyes were wet, he murmured:

"Signora, please…"

His sensitivity touched me, in the midst of my tears I placed the glass on the floor and, as if to console him, I who had need of consolation drew close to him.

He said nothing, but quickly offered me a Kleenex. I whispered some excuse, I was distraught. He wanted to quiet me, he couldn't bear the sight of grief. I dried my eyes, my nose, my mouth, I huddled beside him, finally relief. I rested my head gently on his chest, let an arm fall across his legs. I would never have thought I could do such a thing with a stranger, and burst into tears again. Carrano cautiously, timidly, put an arm around my shoulders. In the house there was a warm silence, I became calm again. I closed my eyes, I was tired and wanted to sleep.

"May I stay like this for a little?" I asked and the answer came almost imperceptibly, almost a breath.

"Yes," he answered, his voice slightly hoarse.

Perhaps I fell asleep. For an instant I had the impression of being in Carla and Mario's room. Above all a strong odor of sex disturbed me. At that hour surely they were still awake, soaking the sheets with sweat, eagerly plunging their tongues into each other's mouth. I started. Something had grazed my neck, maybe Carrano's lips. I looked up in confusion, he kissed me on the mouth.

Today I know what I felt, but then I didn't understand. At that instant I had only an unpleasant impression, as if he had given the signal and from then on all I could do was to sink by degrees into repugnance. In reality I felt above all a blaze of hatred toward myself, because I was there, because I had no excuses, because it was I who had decided to come, because it seemed to me that I could not retreat.

"Shall we begin?" I said with a false cheer.

Carrano gave an uncertain hint of a smile.

"No one is forcing us."

"Do you want to go back?"

"No..."

He again brought his lips to mine, but I didn't like the odor of his saliva, I don't even know if it really was unpleasant, only it seemed to me different from Mario's. He tried to put his tongue in my mouth, I opened my lips a little, touched his tongue with mine. It was slightly rough, alive, it felt animal, an enormous tongue such as I had seen, disgusted, at the butcher, there was nothing seductively human about it. Did Carla have my tastes, my odors? Or had mine always been repellent to Mario, as now Carrano's seemed to me, and only in her, after years, had he found the essences right for him?

I pushed my tongue into the mouth of that man with exaggerated eagerness, for a long time, as if I were following something to the bottom of his throat and wished to catch it before it slid into the esophagus. I put my arm around his neck, I pressed him with my body into the corner of the sofa and kissed him for a long time, with my eyes wide open, trying to stare at the objects arranged in one corner of the room, define them, cling to them, because I was afraid that if I closed my eyes I would see Carla's impudent mouth, she had had that impudence since the age of fifteen, and who could say how much Mario liked it, if he had dreamed of it while he slept beside me, until he woke and kissed me as if he were kissing her and then withdrew and went back to sleep as soon as he recognized my mouth, the usual mouth, the mouth without new tastes, the mouth of the past.

Carrano sensed in my kiss the sign that any skirmishing was over. He put his hand on my neck, he wanted to press me even harder against his lips. Then he left my mouth and planted wet kisses on my cheeks, on my eyes. I thought he must be following a precise exploratory plan, he even kissed my ears, so that the sound echoed annoyingly against my eardrums. Then he moved to my neck, he bathed with his tongue the hair at the nape, and meanwhile he touched my chest with his broad hand.

"My breasts are small," I said in a whisper, but immediately despised myself because it sounded as if I were making excuses, excuse me if I can't offer you big tits, I hope you enjoy yourself anyway, idiot that I was, if he liked little tits, good; if not, the worse for him, it was all free, a stroke of luck had fallen to this shit, the best birthday present he could hope for, at his age.

"I like them," he said in a whisper, while he unbuttoned my shirt and with his hand pulled down the edge of the bra and tried to bite my nipples and suck them. But my nipples, too, are small, and the breasts eluded him, falling back into the cups of the bra. I said wait, I pushed him away, I sat up, I took off the shirt, unhooked the bra. I asked stupidly: do you like them, anxiety was growing in me, I wanted him to repeat his approval.

Looking at me he sighed:

"You're beautiful."

He took a deep breath, as if he wished to control a strong emotion or nostalgia, and just touched me with his fingertips so that I lay on the sofa with my chest bare and he could gaze at me more easily.

Lying there, I saw him from below, I noted the wrinkles of his aging neck, the beard that needed a shave and showed flecks of white, the deep creases between his eyebrows. Perhaps he was serious, perhaps he really was captivated by my beauty, or perhaps they were only words to ornament a desire for sex. Perhaps I remained beautiful even if my husband had rolled up the sense of my beauty into a ball and thrown it into the wastebasket, like wrapping paper. Yes, I could still make a man passionate, I was a woman able to do this, the flight of Mario to another bed, another flesh, had not ruined me.

Carrano bent over me, licked my nipples, sucked them. I tried to abandon myself, I wanted to eliminate disgust and desperation from my breast. I closed my eyes cautiously, the warmth of his breath, the lips on my skin, I let out a moan of encouragement for me and for him. I hoped to notice in myself some nascent pleasure, even if that man was a stranger, a musician perhaps of little talent, no quality, no capacity for seduction, dull and therefore alone.

Now I felt him kissing my ribs, my stomach, he stopped even on my navel, what he found there I don't know, he moved his tongue in it, tickling me. Then he got up. I opened my eyes, he was rumpled, his eyes were bright, I seemed to see in his face the expression of a guilty child.

"Tell me again that you like me," I insisted, short of breath.

"Yes," he said, but with a little less enthusiasm. He put his hands on my knees, parted them, slid his fingers under my skirt, caressed the insides of my thighs, lightly, as if he were sending a probe into the dark depths of a well.

He didn't seem to be in a hurry, I would have preferred everything to proceed more quickly. Now I thought of the possibility that the children might wake up or even of the hypothesis that Mario, after our tumultuous encounter, frightened, repentant, had decided to return home that very night. It even seemed to me that I could hear Otto barking joyfully, and I was about to say the dog is barking, but then it seemed to me inappropriate. Carrano had just raised my skirt and now was caressing the crotch of my underpants with the palm of his hand, and then he ran his fingers over the material pressing, pushing it deep into the fold of my sex.

I moaned again, I wanted to help him take off the underpants, he stopped me.

"No," he said, "wait."

He moved aside the material, caressed my bare sex with his fingers, entered with his index finger, murmured again:

"You're really beautiful."

Beautiful everywhere, outside and in, male fantasies. Was Mario doing that, with me he had never taken his time. But maybe he, too, now, in the long night, somewhere else, was spreading Carla's thin legs, letting his gaze rest on her cunt half covered by the underpants, lingering, his heart pounding, on the obscenity of that position, making it more obscene with his fingers. Or, who knows, maybe it was I alone who was obscene now, abandoned to that man who was touching me in secret places, who, in no hurry, was bathing his fingers inside me, with the casual curiosity of one who isn't in love. Carla, on the other hand—Mario believed this, I was certain that he believed it—was a young woman in love who gives herself to her lover. Not a gesture, not a sigh was vulgar or sordid, not even the coarsest words had any power against the true meaning of their intercourse. I could say cunt and cock and asshole, they were not marked by it. I marked, I disfigured, only my own image on the sofa, what I was at that moment, rumpled, with Carrano's big fingers rousing in me a fund of muddy pleasure.

Again I felt like crying, I clenched my teeth. I didn't know what to do, I didn't want to burst into tears again, I reacted by moving my pelvis, shaking my head, moaning, murmuring:

"You want me, it's true that you want me, tell me…"

Carrano nodded yes, pushed me onto my side, pulled down my underpants. I have to leave, I thought. Now what I wanted to know I knew. I am still attractive to men. Mario took everything but not me, not my person, not my beautiful charming mask. That's enough with my ass. He was biting my buttocks, licking me.

"Not my ass," I said, moving his fingers away. He touched my anus again, I moved him away again. Enough. I drew back, I stretched out a hand toward his bathrobe.

"Let's get it over with," I exclaimed. "Do you have a condom?"

Carrano nodded yes but didn't move. He took his hands off my body, showing a sudden sadness, and leaned his head on the back of the sofa, stared at the ceiling.

"I don't feel anything," he murmured.

"What don't you feel?"

"An erection."

"Never?"

"No, now."

"Since we started?"

"Yes."

I felt myself flare up with shame. He had kissed me, embraced me, touched me, but he hadn't gotten hard, I hadn't been able to make his blood burn, he had roused my flesh without rousing his, ugly shit.

I opened his bathrobe, now I couldn't leave, between the fourth floor and the fifth there were no longer stairs, if I left I would find the abyss.

I looked at his small pallid sex, lost in the black forest of hairs, between the heavy testicles.

"Don't worry," I said, "you're upset."

I jumped up, I took off the skirt that I was still wearing, I was naked, but he didn't even realize it, he continued to look at the ceiling.

"Now you lie down," I ordered him with false calm. "Relax."

I pushed him down on the sofa, supine, in the position in which until that moment I had been.

"Where are the condoms?"

He gave a melancholy smile.

"It's useless at this point," and yet he pointed to a chest of drawers with a gesture of discouragement.

I went to the chest, opened one drawer after another, found the condoms.

"But I was attractive to you..." Again I insisted.

He hit his forehead lightly with the back of his hand.

"Yes, in my mind."

I laughed angrily, I said:

"You have to like me everywhere," and I sat on his chest, turning my back to him. I began to caress his stomach, going slowly lower and lower along the black track of hairs to where they were thick around his sex. Carla was fucking my husband and I couldn't fuck this man, a man alone, without opportunities, a depressed musician for whom I was to be the happy surprise of his fifty-third birthday. She ruled Mario's cock as if it belonged to her, she made him put it in her pussy, in her ass, which he had never done with me, and I, I could only chill that gray flesh. I grabbed his penis, I pulled down the skin to make sure there were no lesions and put it in my mouth. After a while Carrano began to moan, it sounded like braying. Soon his flesh swelled against my palate, this is what the shit wanted, this is what he was waiting for. Finally his prick emerged strong from his belly, a prick to fuck me with, to make my stomach ache for days, as Mario had never fucked me. My husband didn't know what to do with real women: he dared only with whores of twenty, without intelligence, without experience, without teasing words.

Now Carrano was agitated, he told me to wait: wait, wait. I moved backward until I was pressing my sex against his mouth, I left his penis and turned with the most disdainful look I was capable of. "Kiss it," I said, and he kissed me literally, with devotion, I felt the shock of the kiss on my pussy, old fool, the metaphoric language I used with Mario evidently wasn't his, he misunderstood, he didn't realize what I was really ordering him to do, I don't know if Carla was able to decipher my husband's suggestions, I don't know. With my teeth I tore open the condom wrapper, I put it on his prick, come on, get up, I said to him, you like the asshole, deflower me, I never did that with my husband, I want to tell him about it in every detail, put it in my ass.

The musician struggled out from under me, I remained on all fours. I laughed to myself, I couldn't contain myself thinking of Mario's face when I told him. I stopped laughing only when I felt Carrano pushing forcefully against me. I was suddenly afraid, I held my breath. A bestial position, animal liquids and a perfidy utterly human. I turned to look at him, perhaps to beg him not to obey me, to let it go. Our glances met. I don't know what he saw, I saw a man no longer young, with his white bathrobe open, his face shiny with sweat, lips pressed in concentration. I murmured something to him, I don't know what. He unclenched his lips, opened his mouth, closed his eyes. Then he sank down behind me. I supported myself on one side. I saw the whitish stain of semen against the wall of the condom.

"Never mind," I said with a dry explosion of laughter in my throat, and I tore the rubber off his already limp penis, threw it away, it stained the floor with a viscid yellow stripe. "You missed the target."

I put on my clothes, went to the door, he followed me, pulling his bathrobe tight around him. I was disgusted with myself. I murmured before I left:

"It's my fault, I'm sorry."

"No, I'm the one…"

I shook my head, forced a smile, falsely conciliating:

"Putting my ass in your face so boldly: Mario's lover certainly doesn't do that."

I went up the stairs slowly. Crouching in a corner, beside the banister, I saw the *poverella* of so long ago, who said to me in a weary but very serious tone: "I am clean I am true I play with my cards on the table."

In front of the door with its metal plates I kept getting the order of the keys wrong, it was a while before I opened it. When I went inside, I wasted more time locking it. Otto ran up to me cheerfully, I paid no attention, I went to take a shower. I deserved everything that had happened to me, even the harsh words with which I mentally insulted myself, rigid under the spray of the water. I managed to calm myself only by saying aloud: "I love my husband and so all this has meaning." I looked at the clock, it was ten after two, I went to bed and turned out the light. I fell asleep immediately, unexpectedly. I slept with that sentence in my head.

18.

WHEN I OPENED MY EYES AGAIN, five hours later, at seven o'clock on Saturday August 4th, I had trouble getting my bearings. The hardest day of the ordeal of my abandonment was about to begin, but I didn't know it yet.

I reached out a hand toward Mario, I was sure he was sleeping beside me, but beside me there was nothing, not even his pillow, or mine, either. It seemed to me that the bed had grown wider and at the same time shorter. Maybe I've gotten taller, I said to myself, maybe thinner.

I felt sluggish, as if from a circulatory problem, my fingers were swollen. I saw that I hadn't taken off my rings before falling asleep, I hadn't put them on the night table with my habitual gesture. I felt them in the flesh of my ring finger, a chokehold that seemed to me at the origin of the illness in my whole body. With cautious gestures I tried to take them off, I wet my finger with saliva, I couldn't do it. I seemed to have the taste of gold in my mouth.

I was staring at an unfamiliar portion of the ceiling, in front of me was a white wall, not the big closet that I saw every morning. My feet looked out on a void, there was no headboard behind my head. My senses were dulled, between my eardrums and the world, between fingertips and sheets perhaps there was some padding, felt or velvet.

I tried to gather my strength, I raised myself up on my

elbows cautiously, in order not to tear the bed, the room, with the movement, or tear myself, like a label torn from a bottle. With an effort I realized that I must have tossed and turned in my sleep, that I had left my usual corner, that with my absent body I had crawled or rolled through sheets that were wet with sweat. This had never happened before, in general I slept curled up on my side, without changing position. But I couldn't find any other explanation, there were two pillows on my right side and the closet on my left. I fell back exhausted onto the sheets.

At that moment there was a knock at the door. It was Ilaria, she came in with her dress rumpled and a sleepy look, and said:

"Gianni threw up on my bed."

I looked at her obliquely, listlessly, without raising my head. I imagined her old, her features deformed, near death or already dead, and yet a piece of me, the apparition of the child I had been, that I would have been, why that "would have been"? I had swift and faded images in my head, entire sentences, but uttered in a hurry, a whisper. I realized that my grammatical tenses weren't correct, because of that jumbled waking up. Time is a breath, I thought, today it's my turn, in a moment my daughter's, it had happened to my mother, to all my forebears, maybe it was even happening to them and me simultaneously, it will happen.

I decided to get up, but there was a kind of suspension of the order: "get up" remained an intention that hovered idly in my ears. Being a child, then a girl, I waited for a man, now I had lost my husband, I will be unhappy until the moment of death, last night I sucked Carrano's dick out of desperation, to cancel out the insult to my cunt, how much ruined pride.

"I'm coming," I said without moving.

"Why did you sleep in that position?"

"I don't know."

"Gianni put his mouth on my pillow."

"What's wrong with that?"

"He got my bed all dirty and the pillow, too. You have to slap him."

I pulled myself up with an effort of will, I lifted a weight that I hadn't enough strength for. I couldn't seem to take in the fact that it was I myself weighing on me, I weighed more than lead, I had no desire to hold myself up for the whole day. I yawned, I turned my head first to the right and then to the left, I tried again to take off my rings, without success.

"If you don't punish him, I'll pinch you," Ilaria threatened.

I went into the children's room with deliberately slow movements, preceded by my daughter, who, however, was impatient. Otto barked, whined, I heard him scratching at the door that separated the bedrooms from the living room. Gianni was lying on Ilaria's bed, dressed exactly as I had seen him the night before, but sweaty and pale, his eyes closed though he was clearly awake. The light blanket was stained, on the floor a yellowish splotch was spreading.

I said nothing to the child, I didn't need to or feel like it. I went instead to the bathroom, spit in the sink, washed out my mouth. Then I took a rag, I used a cautious gesture, but even that seemed too quick, I had the impression that, against my will, it had made me twist my eyes, pushing them sideways disjointedly, in a sort of forced torsion that threatened to set in motion the wall, the mirror, the chest, everything.

I sighed, a long sigh that was able to fix my pupils on the rag, subduing panic. I returned to the children's room, I squatted down to clean the floor. The acid odor of vomit recalled to me the days of nursing, of baby food, and sudden regurgitations. As I removed the traces of my son's illness from the floor, I thought of the woman of Naples with her whining children, silenced by candies. At a certain point, she, the abandoned wife, began getting angry at them. She said that they had left the odor of motherhood on her, and this had ruined her, it was their fault that her husband had left. First they swell your belly, yes, first they make your breasts heavy, and then they have no patience. Words like that, I recalled. My mother repeated them in a low voice so that I wouldn't hear, gravely agreeing. But I heard them just the same, and now, too, in a sort of double hearing: I was the child of that time playing under the table, stealing sequins, putting them in my mouth, and sucking them; and I was the adult of this morning, here beside Ilaria's bed, mechanically performing a dirty job and yet sensitive to the sound of the sticky rag sliding over the floor. How had Mario been? Tender, it seemed to me, with no outward signs of impatience or annoyance with my pregnancies. In fact, when I was pregnant he wanted to make love more often, and I did it more willingly. Now I was cleaning, and meanwhile I made mental calculations, numbers without emotion. Ilaria had been a year and a half when Carla appeared in our life, and Gianni less than five. I had had no work, any sort of work, even writing, for at least five years. I lived in a new city, still a new city, I had no relatives to ask for help, and even if I had I wouldn't have asked, I wasn't a person who asks for help. I did the shopping, I cooked, I cleaned, I took the two children from place to place, from room to room, exhausted, exasperated. I dealt with deadlines of every sort, I took care of the income taxes, I ran to the bank, ran to the post office. At night I wrote down, in my notebooks, income and expenses, in every detail, as if I were an accountant who had to show the books to the owner of the business. At times I also wrote, between the numbers, how I felt: I was like a lump of food that my children chewed without stopping; a cud made of a living material that continually amalgamated and softened its living substance to allow two greedy bloodsuckers to nourish themselves, leaving on me the odor and taste of their gastric juices. Nursing, how repulsive, an animal function. And then the warm sweetish odor of baby-food breath. No matter how much I washed, that stink of motherhood remained. Sometimes Mario pasted himself against me, took me, holding me as I nearly slept, tired himself after work, without emotions. He did it persisting on my almost absent flesh that tasted of milk, cookies, cereal, with a desperation of his own that overlapped mine without his realizing it. I was the body of incest, I thought, stunned by the odor of Gianni's vomit, I was the mother to be violated, not a lover. Already he was searching elsewhere for figures more suitable for love, fleeing the sense of guilt, and he became melancholy, sighed. Carla had happened into the house at the right moment, a figment of unsatisfied desire. She was then thirteen years older than Ilaria, ten more than Gianni, seven more than me when I heard my mother speaking of the *poverella* of Piazza Mazzini. Mario must have imagined her as the future, and yet he desired the past, the girlhood that I had already given him and that he now felt nostalgia for. She herself perhaps believed she was giving him the future and had encouraged him to believe it. But we were all confused, especially me. While I was taking care of the children, I was expecting from Mario a moment that never arrived, the moment when I would be again as I had been before my pregnancies, young, slender, energetic, shamelessly certain I could make of myself a memorable person. No, I thought, squeezing the rag and struggling to get up: starting at a certain point, the future is only a need to live in the past. To immediately redo the grammatical tenses.

19.

"THAT'S GROSS," SAID ILARIA, and cringed with exaggerated disgust, as I went by with the rag to wash it in the bathroom. I said to myself that if I devoted myself immediately to the usual domestic activities I would be better off. Do the laundry. Separate the white clothes from the dark. Start the washing machine. I had only to quiet the view inside, the thoughts. They got mixed up, they crowded in on one another, shreds of words and images, buzzing frantically, like a swarm of wasps, they gave to my gestures a brute capacity to do harm. I washed the rag carefully, then soaped around the rings, the wedding ring and an aquamarine that had been my mother's. Very slowly I managed to get them off, but it didn't do me any good, my body remained obstructed, the knots in the veins didn't loosen. Mechanically I placed the rings on the edge of the sink.

When I returned to the children's room, I leaned absently over Gianni to feel his forehead with my lips. He groaned and said:

"My head feels terrible."

"Get up," I ordered, unsympathetically, and he, staring at me in wonder because of my scant attention to his complaints, struggled to get up. I stripped the bed with false calm, I remade it, I put the sheets and pillowcases in the dirty-laundry basket. Only then did I remember to say to him:

"Get in bed, I'll bring the thermometer."

Ilaria insisted:

"You have to slap him."

When I began to search for the thermometer without satisfying her request, she punished me with a sudden pinch, observed me closely to see if it hurt.

I didn't react, it didn't matter to me, I felt nothing. She persisted, red in the face from effort and concentration. When I found the thermometer, I pushed her away with a slight shove of the elbow and went back to Gianni. I stuck the thermometer under his armpit.

"Tight," I said, and indicated the clock on the wall. "Take it out in ten minutes."

"You put it in wrong," said Ilaria in a provocative tone.

I didn't pay any attention to her, but Gianni checked and with a look of reproof showed me that I had put the side without the mercury under his armpit. Attention: attention alone could help me. I put it in correctly, Ilaria appeared satisfied, she said: I noticed it. I nodded yes, good, I made a mistake. Why—I thought—must I do a thousand things at once, for almost ten years you've been forcing me to live like this, and I'm not completely awake yet, I haven't had my coffee, I haven't made breakfast.

I wanted to put the coffee in the pot and get it on the stove, I wanted to warm milk for Ilaria, I wanted to start the washing machine. But suddenly I noticed Otto's barking again, he hadn't stopped and was scratching. I had removed those sounds from my ears in order to concentrate on the condition of my son, but now the dog seemed to be producing not sounds but electric shocks.

"I'm coming," I cried.

The evening before—I realized—I hadn't taken him out, I had forgotten, and the dog must have been yelping all night, now he was wild, he had his needs to take care of. And I did, too. I was a sack of living flesh, packed with waste, bladder bursting, stomach aching. I thought it without a shadow of self-pity, as a cold statement. The chaotic sounds in my head struck decisive blows on the sack that I was: he vomited, I have a headache, where is the thermometer, bowwowwow, react.

"I'm taking the dog out," I said loudly to myself.

I put the collar on Otto, I turned the key, I struggled to get it out of the lock. Only on the stairs did I realize that I was in my nightgown and slippers. I realized it as I passed Carrano's door, I grimaced with a laugh of disgust, surely he was sleeping, recovering from the night's exertions. What did he matter to me, he had seen me in my true self, my body of a nearly forty-year-old, we were very intimate. As for the other neighbors, they had been on vacation for a while already or had left Friday afternoon for a weekend in the mountains, at the sea. The three of us, too, would have been settled at least a month earlier at some seaside vacation place, as we were every year, if Mario hadn't left. The lech. Empty building, August was like that. I felt like guffawing at every door, sticking out my tongue, thumbing my nose. I didn't give a shit about them. Happy little families, good money from professions, comfort constructed by selling at a high price services that should be free. Like Mario, who allowed us to live well by selling his ideas, his intelligence, the persuasive tones of his voice when he taught. Ilaria called to me from the landing:

"I don't want to stay with the vomit stink."

When I didn't answer, she went back inside, I heard the door slam furiously. But good Lord, if someone was pulling me from one side I couldn't be pulled from the other, too, what's here isn't there. In fact, Otto, panting, was dragging me rapidly from one flight of stairs to the next, connecting them, while I tried to hold him back. I didn't want to run, if I ran I would break, every step left behind disintegrated immediately afterward, even in memory, and the banister, the yellow wall rushed by me fluidly, cascading. I saw only the flights of stairs, with their clear segments, behind me was a gassy wake, I was a comet. Oh what a terrible day, too hot already at seven in the morning, not a car in sight except Carrano's and mine. Maybe I was too tired to maintain the usual order of the world. I shouldn't have gone out. What had I done? Had I put the coffeepot on the stove? Had I put in the coffee, filled it with water? Had I screwed it tight so that it wouldn't explode? And the milk for the child? Were they actions that I had completed or had I only suggested to myself that I complete them? Open the refrigerator, get out the carton of milk, close the refrigerator, fill the pan, don't leave the carton on the table, put it back in the fridge, light the gas, put the pot on the fire. Had I correctly carried out all those operations?

Otto pulled me along the path, through the tunnel with its obscene graffiti. The park was deserted, the river seemed of blue plastic, the hills on the other bank were of a diluted green, no noise of traffic, only the song of the birds could be heard. I had left the coffee on the stove, and the milk, it would all be burned. The milk, boiling up, would overflow the pot and put out the flame, gas would spread through the house. Still the obsession with gas. I hadn't opened the windows. Or had I done it automatically, without thinking? Habitual acts, they are performed in the head even when you don't perform them. Or you perform them in reality, even when the head out of habit has stopped taking account of them. I listed possibilities, distractedly. Better if I had locked myself in the bathroom, my stomach was bursting, I felt a painful pressure. The sun outlined the leaves of the trees minutely, even the needles of the pines, in a maniacal work of the light, I could count them one by one. No, I hadn't put either the coffee or the milk on the stove. Now I was sure of it. Preserve that certainty. Good, Otto.

Pushed by his needs, the dog obliged me to run behind him, my stomach pressed by mine. The leash was grazing the palm of my hand, I gave a fierce tug, I bent down to free him. He ran away like pure life, a dark mass charged with urgencies. He watered trees, shit in the grass, chased butterflies, lost himself in the pine grove. When was it that I had lost that stubborn charge of animal energy, with adolescence, perhaps. Now I was wild again, I looked at my ankles, my armpits, when had I last waxed them, when had I shaved? I who until four months ago had been only ambrosia and nectar? From the moment I fell in love with Mario, I began to fear that he would be repelled by me. Wash the body, scent it, eliminate all unpleasant traces of physiology. To levitate. I wanted to detach myself from the earth, I wanted him to see me hovering on high, the way wholly good things do. I never left the bathroom until every bad smell had vanished, I turned on the taps so he wouldn't hear the rush of urine. I rubbed myself, curried myself, washed my hair every two days. I thought of beauty as of a constant effort to eliminate corporeality. I wanted him to love my body forgetful of what one knows of bodies. Beauty, I thought anxiously, is this forgetfulness. Or maybe not. It was I who believed that his love needed that obsession of mine. Inappropriate, backward, my mother's fault, she had trained me in the obsessive bodily attentions of women. I don't know whether I was repelled or amazed or even entertained, when the young woman, twenty-five at most, who had long been my office mate when I worked for an airline company, one morning farted without embarrassment and, with laughing eyes, gave me a half smile of complicity. Girls now burped in public, farted, in fact—I recalled—one of my school friends did it, she was seventeen, three years younger than Carla. She wanted to be a ballerina and she passed the time practicing ballet positions. She was good. During recess she pirouetted lightly around the classroom, skirting the desks with precision. Then, to scandalize us, or to disfigure the image of elegance that remained in the boys' doltish eyes, she made bodily noises according to how she felt, with her throat, her ass. The ferocity of women, I had felt it in me since waking, in my flesh. Suddenly I was afraid I would dissolve into liquid, a fear that gripped my stomach, I had to sit down on a bench, hold my breath. Otto had disappeared, perhaps he had no intention of ever returning, I whistled weakly, he was in the thick of nameless trees, which seemed to me more like a watercolor than like reality. The ones beside me, behind me. Poplars? Cedars? Acacias? Locusts? Names at random, what did I know, I didn't know anything, even the names of the trees outside my house. If I had had to write about them, I would have been unable to. The trunks all seemed to be under a powerful magnifying lens. There was no distance between me and them, whereas the rules say that to tell a story you need first of all a measuring stick, a calendar, you have to calculate how much time has passed, how much space has been interposed between you and the facts, the emotions to be narrated. But I felt everything right on top of me, breath against breath. And then it seemed to me that I was wearing not my nightgown but a long mantle on which was painted the vegetation of the Valentino, the paths, the Princess Isabella bridge, the river, the building where I lived, even the dog. That was why I was so heavy and swollen. I got up groaning with embarrassment and stomachache, my bladder full, I couldn't hold it any longer. I stumbled in a zigzag, clutching the house keys, hitting the ground with the leash. No, I knew nothing of trees. A poplar? A cedar of Lebanon? A pine of Aleppo? What's the difference between an acacia and a locust? Tricks of words, a swindle, maybe the promised land has no more words to embellish the facts. Smiling scornfully—with scorn for myself—I pulled up my nightgown, I peed and shit behind a trunk. I was tired, tired, tired.

I said it loudly but voices die quickly, they seem alive in the bottom of the throat and yet, if articulated, they are already spent sounds. I heard Ilaria calling from very far away. Her words reached me faintly.

"Mamma, come back, Mamma."

They were the words of an agitated creature. I couldn't see

her, but I imagined that she had uttered them with her hands clutched tight around the railing of the balcony. I knew that the long platform extending over a void frightened her, she must really need me if she had gotten herself out there. Maybe the milk really was burning on the stove, maybe the coffeepot had exploded, maybe gas was spreading through the house. But why should I hurry? I discovered with remorse that, if the child needed me, I felt no need of her. Nor did Mario, either. That was why he had gone to live with Carla, he didn't need Ilaria, or Gianni. Desire cuts off. Maybe it only cuts. His desire had been to skate far away from us on an infinite surface; mine, it seemed to me now, was to go to the bottom, abandon myself, sink deaf and mute into my own veins, into my intestine, my bladder. I realized that I was covered in a cold sweat, a frozen patina, even though the morning was already hot. What was happening to me. It was impossible that I would ever find the way home.

But at that point something brushed against my ankle, wetting it. I saw Otto beside me, his ears pricked, his tongue hanging out, the gaze of a good dog. I rose, I tried to put the collar on, again and again, without success, even when he stood still, barely panting, with an odd look, sad, maybe. Finally, with an effort of concentration, I imprisoned his neck. Go, go, I said to him. It seemed to me that if I were behind him, holding tight to the leash, I would feel again the warm air on my face, my skin dry, the ground beneath my feet.

20.

I ARRIVED AT THE ELEVATOR as if I had walked on a wire stretched between the pine grove and the entrance to the building. I leaned against the metal wall while the car slowly rose, I stared at Otto to thank him. He stood with his legs slightly apart, he was panting and a thread of saliva dripped from his jaws, making a squiggle on the floor of the elevator. The car jolted as it came to a stop.

On the landing I found Ilaria, she seemed to me very annoyed, as if she were my mother returned from the kingdom of the dead to remind me of my duties.

"He threw up again," she said.

She preceded me into the house, followed by Otto, whom I freed from the leash. No smell of burned milk, of coffee. I slowed down to close the door, mechanically I put the keys in the locks, gave the two turns. My hand was used by now to that movement which was to keep anyone from entering my house to search among my things. I had to protect myself from those who would do their utmost to load me with obligations, guilts, and keep me from starting to live again. I was struck by the suspicion that even my children wanted to convince me that their flesh was withering because of me, just from breathing the same air. Gianni's illness served this purpose. He set the scene, Ilaria flung it eagerly in my face. More vomit, yes, and so? It wasn't the first time, it wouldn't be the last. Gianni, like his father, had a weak stomach. They both suffered from sea-sickness, carsickness. A sip of cold water sufficed, a slice of too rich cake, and they felt sick. Who knows what the boy had secretly eaten, to complicate my life, to make the day more arduous for me.

The room was again in disarray. Now the dirty sheets were in a corner, like a cloud, and Gianni had gone back to Ilaria's bed. The child had replaced me. She had behaved the way I had behaved as a girl with my mother: she had tried to do what she had seen me do, she was playing at getting rid of my authority by supplanting me, she wanted to take my place. In general I was accommodating, my mother had not been. Every time I tried to do something like her, she rebuked me, she said I had been bad. Maybe it was she in person who was acting through the child to crush me with the demonstration of my inadequacy. Ilaria explained, as if inviting me to join a game in which she was the queen:

"I put the dirty sheets there and I made him lie on my bed. He didn't throw up much, he only did like this."

She staged some retching actions, then spit several times on the floor.

I went to Gianni, he was sweating, he looked at me with hostility.

"Where's the thermometer?" I asked.

Ilaria took it promptly from the night table and offered it to me, pretending information she didn't have, she didn't know how to read it.

"He has a fever," she said, "but he doesn't want to take a suppository."

I looked at the thermometer, I couldn't concentrate on the degrees indicated by the column of mercury. I don't know how long I remained with that object in my hand anxiously trying to train my gaze to see. I have to take care of the child, I said to myself, I have to know how high the fever is, but I couldn't pay attention. Certainly something had happened to me during the night. Or after months of tension I had arrived at the edge of some precipice and now I was falling, as in a dream, slowly, even as I continued to hold the thermometer in my hand, even as I stood with the soles of my slippers on the floor, even as I felt myself solidly contained by the expectant looks of my children. It was the fault of the torture that my husband had inflicted. But enough, I had to tear the pain from memory, I had to sandpaper away the scratches that were damaging my brain. Remove the other dirty sheets. Put them in the washing machine. Start it. Stand and watch through the window, the clothes rotating, the water and soap.

"It's a hundred and one," said Gianni in a whisper, "and my head feels terrible."

"He has to take the suppository," Ilaria insisted.

"I won't take it."

"Then I'll hit you," the girl threatened.

"You aren't going to hit anyone," I intervened.

"Why do you hit us?"

I didn't hit them, I had never done it, at most I had threatened to do it. But maybe for children there's no difference between what one threatens and what one really does. At least—I now remembered—as a child I had been like that, maybe also as an adult. What might happen if I violated a prohibition of my mother's happened anyway, independent of the violation. The words immediately made the future real, and the wound of the punishment still burned even when I no longer remembered the fault that I would or could have committed. A recurrent expression of my mother's came to mind. "Stop or I'll cut off your hands," she would say when I touched her dressmaking things. And those words were a pair of long, burnished steel scissors that came out of her mouth, jawlike blades that closed over the wrists, leaving stumps sewed up with a needle and thread from her spools.

"I've never hit you," I said.

"That's not true."

"At most I've said I would slap you. There's quite a difference."

There's no difference, I thought, however, and hearing that thought in my head scared me. Because if I lost the capacity to perceive a difference, if I lost it definitively, if I ended up in an alluvial flow that eliminated boundaries, what would happen on that hot day?

"When I say 'slap,' I'm not slapping you," I explained to her calmly, as if I were before an examiner and wished to make a good showing, presenting myself as cool and rational. "The word 'slap' is not this slap."

And not so much to convince her as to convince me, I slapped myself hard. Then I smiled, not only because that slap suddenly seemed to me objectively comical but also to show that my demonstration was lighthearted, unthreatening. It was no use. Gianni quickly covered his face with the sheet and Ilaria looked at me in amazement, her eyes suddenly full of tears.

"You hurt yourself, Mamma," she said woefully. "Your nose is bleeding."

Blood was dripping on my nightgown, and I felt somehow ashamed.

I sniffed, I went into the bathroom, I locked the door to keep the child from following me. All right, concentrate, Gianni has a fever, do something. I stopped the blood by sticking some cotton in one nostril and immediately began digging nervously among the medicines that I had put in order the night before. I wanted to find something for his fever, but meanwhile I thought: I need a tranquilizer, something bad is happening to me, I have to calm down, and I felt at the same time that Gianni, the memory of Gianni feverish in the other room, was slipping away from me, I couldn't maintain the glimmer of worry about his health, already the child was becoming indifferent to me, it was as if I saw him only out of the corner of my eye, a misty figure, a fraying cloud.

I began to look for pills for myself, but there were none, where had I put them, in the sink the night before, I remembered suddenly, how stupid. Then I thought of having a hot bath to relax, and maybe waxing, a bath would be soothing, I need the weight of water on my skin, I'm losing myself and if I don't catch hold what will happen to the children?

I didn't want Carla to touch them, the mere idea gave me shivers of disgust. A girl taking care of my children, she isn't completely out of adolescence, her hands are smeared with the semen of her lover, the same seed that is in the blood of the children. Keep them far away, therefore, her and Mario. Be self-sufficient, accept nothing from them. I began to fill the tub, sound of the first drops hitting the bottom, hypnotic effect of the stream from the tap.

But I no longer heard the rush of water, now I was getting lost in the mirror that was next to me, I saw myself, I saw myself with an unbearable clarity, the disheveled hair, the eyes without makeup, the swollen nose with its blood-blackened cotton, the entire face clawed by a grimace of concentration, the short, stained nightgown.

I wanted to remedy this. I began to clean my face with a cotton ball, I wished to be beautiful again, I felt an urgent need for it. Beauty brightens things, the children would be glad, Gianni would draw from it a pleasure that would cure him, I myself would be better. Delicate makeup remover for the eyes, gentle cleansing milk, hydrating tonic without alcohol, foundation, makeup. What is a face without colors, to color is to conceal, there is nothing that can hide the surface better than color. Go, go, go. From deep down rose the murmur of voices, Mario's voice. I slid behind my husband's words of love, words of years ago. Little bird of a happy and contented life, he said to me, because he was a good reader of the classics and had an enviable memory. And with amusement he made a list: he wanted to be my bra so he could hug my chest, and my underpants and my skirt and the shoe stepped on by my foot, and the water that washed me and the cream that rubbed me and the mirror in which I looked at myself; ironic toward good literature, he was an engineer playing with my mania for beautiful words and at the same time charmed by the gift of so many images ready to give form to the desire he felt for me, for me, the woman in the mirror. A mask of lipstick and blush, nose swollen by cotton, the taste of blood in my throat.

I turned with a gesture of repulsion, in time to realize that the water was overflowing the tub. I turned off the tap. I stuck a hand in, cold water, I hadn't even checked to see if it was warm. My face slid away from the mirror, it no longer interested me. The sensation of cold restored me to Gianni's fever, his vomiting, his headache. What was I looking for, locked in the bathroom: the aspirin. I began to search again, I found it, I cried as if for help:

"Ilaria? Gianni?"

21.

NOW I FELT A NEED for their voices, but they didn't answer. I rushed to the door, tried to open it, couldn't. The key, I remembered, but I turned it to the right, as if to lock it, instead of to the left. I took a deep breath, remembered the gesture, turned the key in the proper direction, went into the hall.

Otto was in front of the door. He was lying on one side, his head resting on the floor. He didn't move when he saw me, he didn't even prick up his ears, or wag his tail. I knew that position, he assumed it when he was suffering for some reason, and wanted attention, it was the pose of melancholy and pain, it meant he was looking for understanding. Stupid dog, he, too, wanted to convince me that I was spreading anxieties. Was I dispensing spores of illness throughout the house? Was it possible? For how long, four, five years? Was that why Mario had turned to little Carla? I rested one bare foot on the dog's stomach, I felt its heat devour my sole, rise to my guts. I saw that a lacework of drool ornamented his jaws.

"Gianni's sleeping," Ilaria whispered from the end of the hall. "Come here."

I climbed over the dog, went into the children's room.

"How pretty you look," Ilaria exclaimed with sincere admiration, and pushed me toward Gianni to show me how he was sleeping. The child had on his forehead three coins and in fact he was sleeping, breathing heavily.

"The coins are cool," Ilaria explained. "They make the headache and fever go away."

Every so often she removed one and put it in a glass of water, then dried it and placed it again on her brother's forehead.

"When he wakes up he has to take an aspirin," I said.

I placed the box on the night table, returned to the hall to occupy myself with something, anything. Get breakfast, yes. But Gianni shouldn't have any food. The washing machine. Even pat Otto. But I realized that the dog was no longer in front of the bathroom door, he had decided to stop displaying his slobbering melancholy. Just as well. If my noxious existence wasn't communicating itself to others, to creatures human and animal, then it was the illness of the others that was invading me and making me sick. Therefore—I thought as if it were a decisive act—a doctor was needed. I had to telephone.

I compelled myself to hold onto this thought, I dragged it behind me like a ribbon in the wind, and so went cautiously into the living room. I was struck by the disorder of my desk. The drawers were open, there were books scattered here and there. Even the notebook in which I made notes for my book was open. I leafed through the last pages. I found transcribed there in my tiny handwriting some passages from *Woman Destroyed* and a few lines from *Anna Karenina*. I didn't remember having done this. Of course, it was a habit of mine to copy passages from books, but not in that notebook, I had a notebook specifically for that. Was it possible that my memory was breaking down? Nor did I remember having drawn firm lines in red ink under the questions that Anna asks herself a little before the train hits her and runs her over: "Where am I? What am I doing? Why?" The passages didn't surprise me, I seemed to know them well, yet I didn't understand what they were doing in those pages. Did I know them so well because I had transcribed them recently, yesterday, the day before? But then why didn't I remember having done it? Why were they in that notebook and not the other?

I sat down at the desk. I had to hold on to something, but I could no longer remember what. Nothing was solid, everything was slipping away. I stared at my notebook, the red lines under Anna's questions like a mooring. I read and reread, but my eyes ran over the questions without understanding. Something in my senses wasn't working. An interruption of feeling, of feelings. Sometimes I abandoned myself to it, at times I was frightened. Those words, for example: I didn't know how to find answers to the question marks, every possible answer seemed absurd. I was lost in the where am I, in the what am I doing. I was mute beside the why. This I had become in the course of a night. Maybe, I didn't know when, after protesting, after resisting for months, I had seen myself in those books and I was in bad shape, definitively broken. A broken clock that, because its metal heart continued to beat, was now breaking the time of everything else.

22.

AT THAT POINT I felt a tickle in my nostrils, I thought that my nose was bleeding again. I soon realized that I had taken for a tactile impression what was an olfactory wound. A thick poisonous odor was spreading through the house. I thought that Gianni must be really sick, I pulled myself together, went back to his room. But the child was still sleeping, in spite of his sister's assiduous changing of the coins on his forehead. Then I moved slowly through the hall, cautiously, toward Mario's study. The door was half open, I entered.

The bad smell was coming from there, the air was unbreatheable. Otto was lying on his side, under his master's desk. When I approached him, he shuddered through his whole body. Saliva dripped from his jaws but his eyes were those of a good dog, even though they looked white, as if bleached. A blackish stain was spreading next to him, dark mud veined with blood.

At first I thought of backing off, leaving the room, closing the door. For a long time I hesitated, taking in that new strange creeping of the illness through my house, what was happening. In the end I decided to stay. The dog was lying mutely, no spasm shook him, his eyelids were lowered now. He seemed to be immobilized in a final contraction, as if he were wound tight, like one of those metal toys of long ago, ready to start up suddenly, as soon as you lowered a little lever with your finger.

Very slowly I got used to the room's offensive odor, I accepted it to the point where, after a few seconds, its surface was torn in several places and another odor began to seep through, for me even more offensive, the odor that Mario hadn't taken away and which was stationed there, in his study. How long since I had entered that room? As soon as possible, I thought angrily, I had to make him take everything out of the apartment, clear himself out of every corner. He couldn't decide to leave me and yet store in the house the perspiration from his pores, the aura of his body, so strong that it broke even the poisonous seal of Otto. Besides—I realized—it was that odor which had given the dog the energy to lower the door handle with his paw and, similarly dissatisfied with me, drag himself under the desk, in that room where the traces of his master were more intense and promised him relief.

I felt humiliated, even more humiliated than I had felt in all these months. A dog without gratitude, I had taken care of him, I had stayed without abandoning him, I had taken him outside for his needs, and he, now that he was becoming a terrain of sores and sweat, went to find comfort among the scents of my husband, the untrustable, the traitor, the deserter. Stay here by yourself, I thought, you deserve it. I didn't know what was wrong with him, it didn't even matter to me, he, too, was a flaw in my awakening, an incongruous event in a day that I was unable to put in order. I backed up angrily toward the door, in time to hear Ilaria behind me asking:

"What stinks?"

Then she glimpsed Otto lying under the desk and she asked: "Is he sick, too? Did he eat poison?"

"What poison?" I asked as I closed the door.

"The poisoned dog biscuits. Daddy always says you have to be careful. The man downstairs who hates dogs puts them in the park."

She tried to reopen the door, fearful for Otto, but I prevented her.

"He's fine," I said. "He just has a little stomachache."

She looked at me very closely, so that I thought she wanted to figure out if I was telling her the truth. Instead she asked:

"Can I make myself up like you?"

"No. Take care of your brother."

"You take care of him," she retorted in irritation and went toward the bathroom.

"Ilaria, don't touch my makeup."

She didn't answer and I let her go, I let her go, that is, beyond the corner of my eye, I didn't even turn, I went dragging my feet to Gianni's room. I felt exhausted, even my voice seemed to me more a sound in my mind than a reality. I took Ilaria's coins off his forehead, I ran my hand over his dry skin. It was burning.

"Gianni," I called, but he continued to sleep or pretend to sleep. His mouth was half open, his lips inflamed like a fiery red wound in the middle of which shone his teeth. I didn't know whether to touch him again, kiss his forehead, shake him lightly to try to wake him. I repressed also the question of the gravity of his illness: food poisoning, a summer flu, the effect of a frozen drink, meningitis. Everything seemed possible, or impossible, and yet I had trouble forming hypotheses, I was unable to establish hierarchies, above all I couldn't get alarmed. Now, instead, thoughts in themselves frightened me, I would have liked not to have any more, I felt they were infected. After seeing Otto's condition, I was even more afraid of being the channel of every evil, better to avoid contacts, Ilaria, I mustn't touch her. The best thing was to call the doctor, an old pediatrician, and the vet. Had I already done it? Had I thought of doing it and then forgotten? Call them right away, that was the rule, respect it. Even though it annoyed me to act as Mario had always acted. Hypochondriac. He got worried, he called the doctor for a trifle. Dad knows—the children, besides, had always pointed out to me—he knows that the man downstairs puts poisoned dog biscuits in the park; he knows what to do about a high fever, about a headache, about symptoms of poison; he knows that you need a doctor, he knows you need the vet. If he had been present—I sobbed—he would have called a doctor for me above all. But I immediately removed that idea of solicitude attributed to a man from whom I solicited nothing anymore. I was an obsolete wife, a cast-off body, my illness is only female life that has outlived its usefulness. I headed decisively toward the telephone. Call the vet, call the doctor. I picked up the receiver.

I put it down immediately in anger.

Where was I with my head?

Collect myself, take hold of myself.

The receiver gave the usual stormy whistle, no line. I knew it and pretended not to know it. Or I didn't know it, my memory had lost its ability to grip, I was no longer capable of learning, of retaining what I had learned, and yet I pretended that I was still capable, I pretended and I avoided responsibility for the children, the dog, with the cold pantomime of one who knows and does.

I picked up the receiver, dialed the number of the pediatrician. Nothing, the whistling continued. I got down on my knees, I looked for the plug under the table, I unplugged it, plugged it back in. I tried the telephone again: the whistling. I dialed the number: the whistling. Then I began to blow into the receiver myself, stubbornly, as if with my breath I could chase away that wind that was canceling my line. No success. I gave up on the telephone, returned idly to the hall. Maybe I hadn't understood, I had to make an effort to concentrate, I had to take in the fact that Gianni was ill, that Otto, too, was ill, I had to find a way of feeling alarm for their condition, grasp what it meant. I counted on the tips of my fingers, diligently. One, there was the telephone not working in the living room; two, there was a child with a high fever and vomiting in his room; three, there was a German shepherd in bad shape in Mario's study. But without getting agitated, Olga, without rushing. Pay attention, in the excitement you might forget your arm, your voice, a thought. Or tear the floor, permanently separate the living room from the children's room. I asked Gianni, perhaps shaking him too hard:

"How are you feeling?"

The child opened his eyes.

"Call Daddy."

Enough of your useless father.

"I'm here, don't worry."

"Yes, but call Daddy."

Daddy wasn't there, Daddy who knew what to do had left. We had to manage by ourselves. But the telephone didn't work, disturbance in the line. And maybe I was leaving, too, for an instant I had a clear awareness of it. I was leaving on unknowable pathways, pathways leading me farther astray, not leading me out, the child had understood, and he was worried not so much about his headache, his fever, as about me. About me.

This hurt me. Remedy it, stay back from the edge. On the table I saw a metal clip for holding scattered papers together. I took it, I clipped it on the skin of my right arm, it might be useful. Something to hold me.

"I'll be right back," I said to Gianni, and he pulled himself up a little to look at me better.

"What did you do to your nose?" he asked. "All that cotton's going to hurt you, take it out. And why did you put that thing on your arm? Stay with me."

He had looked at me carefully. But what had he seen. The wadding, the clip. Not a word about my makeup, he hadn't found me pretty. Males small or big are unable to appreciate true beauty, they think only of their own needs. Later, of course, he would desire his father's lover. Probably. I went out of the room, went into Mario's study. I adjusted the metal clip. Was it possible that Otto really had been poisoned, that Carrano was responsible for the poison?

The dog was still there, under his master's desk. The smell was unbearable, he had had another bout of diarrhea. But now there was not only him in the room. Behind the desk, on my husband's swivel chair, in the gray-blue shadows, sat a woman.

23.

SHE WAS RESTING her bare feet on Otto's body, she was green-ish in color, she was the abandoned woman of Piazza Mazzini, the *poverella*, as my mother called her. She smoothed her hair carefully, as if she were combing it with her hands, and adjust-ed over her bosom her faded dress, which was too low-cut. Her appearance lasted long enough to take away my breath, then she vanished.

A bad sign. I was frightened, I felt that the hours of the hot day were pushing me where I absolutely should not go. If the woman was really in the room, I reflected, I, in consequence, must be a child of eight. Or worse: if that woman was there, a child of eight, who was by now alien to me, was getting the best of me, who was thirty-eight, and was imposing her time, her world. This child was working to remove the ground from beneath my feet and replace it with her own. And it was only the beginning: if I were to help her, if I were to abandon myself, I felt, then, that day and the very space of the apartment would be open to many different times, to a crowd of environments and persons and things and selves who, simultaneously present, would offer real events, dreams, nightmares, to the point of cre-ating a labyrinth so dense that I would never get out of it.

I wasn't naïve, I mustn't allow this. It was necessary not to forget that the woman behind the desk, although a bad sign, was still a sign. Shake yourself, Olga. No woman of flesh and blood had entered whole into my child's head; no woman of flesh and blood could now get out of it, whole. The person I had just seen behind Mario's desk was only an effect of the word "woman," "woman of Piazza Mazzini," "the *poverella*." Therefore hold on to these notions: the dog is alive, for now; the woman, however, is dead, drowned three decades ago; I stopped being a girl of eight thirty years ago. To remind myself of it I bit my knuckle for a long time, until I felt pain. Then I sank into the sick stench of the dog, I wanted to smell only that.

I knelt beside Otto. He was racked by uncontrollable spasms, the dog had become a puppet in the hands of suffering. What I had before my eyes. His jaws were locked, the drool thick. Those contractions of his limbs seemed to me finally a hold more solid than the bite on my knuckle, than the clip pinching my arm.

I have to do something, I thought. Ilaria is right: Otto has been poisoned, it's my fault, I didn't watch him carefully.

But the thought was unable to feint around the usual wrapping of my voice. I felt in my throat, as if I were speaking inside it, a vibration of breath that was like a baby's, adult and at the same time affectedly girlish, a tone that I have always detested. Carla's voice was like that, I recalled: at fifteen she had sounded like six, perhaps she still did. How many women can't give up the pretense of the childish voice. I had given it up immediately, at ten I was already searching for adult tonalities. Not even in moments of love had I ever sounded childish. A woman is a woman.

"Go to Carrano," the *poverella* of Piazza Mazzini advised me in a strong Neapolitan accent, reappearing this time in a corner near the window. "Get him to help you."

I couldn't stop myself, I seemed to complain with the thin voice of a child exposed to danger, innocent when everything is harmful to her:

"Carrano poisoned Otto. He promised Mario. The most innocuous people are capable of doing terrible things."

"But also good things, my child. Go on, he's the only one in the building, he's the only one who can help you."

What an idiot, I should absolutely not have spoken to her. A dialogue, in fact. As if I were writing my book and had in my head phantom people, characters. But I wasn't writing, nor was I under my mother's table telling myself the story of the *poverella*. I was talking to myself. That's how it begins, you answer your own words as if they belonged to someone else. What a mistake. I had to anchor myself to things, accept their solidity, believe in their permanence. The woman was present only in my childhood memories. I mustn't be frightened, but I also mustn't encourage her. We carry in our head until we die the living and the dead. The essential thing is to impose a balance, for example never speak to your own words. In order to know where I was, who I was, I stuck both hands into Otto's fur, from which an unbearable heat emanated. As soon as I touched it, as soon as I petted him, he started, raised his head, opened his white eyes wide, spit out at me bits of saliva, growling. I retreated, frightened. The dog didn't want me in his suffering, he pushed me back into mine as if I didn't deserve to alleviate his agony.

The woman said:

"You haven't much time. Otto is dying."

24.

I GOT UP, I hurried out of the room, closing the door behind me. I would have liked to have giant strides that would not allow me to stop for anything. Olga marches down the hall, through the living room. She is decisive now, she will remedy things, even if the girl she has in her head is speaking to her in sugary tones, says to her: Ilaria has taken your makeup, who knows what she's up to in the bathroom, your things are no longer really yours, she's touching everything, go and slap her. Yet I slowed down immediately, I couldn't tolerate excitement, if the world around me accelerated I decelerated. Olga has a terror of the frenzy of doing, she fears that the need for a prompt reaction—quick steps, quick gestures—will migrate into her brain, she can't tolerate the inner roar that will assault her, the pounding temples, the nausea, the cold sweat, the craze to be faster and faster, faster and faster. So no hurry, take your time, walk slowly, shuffle, even. Reset the bite of the clip on my arm to get me to abandon that third person, the Olga who wanted to run, and return to the I, I who go to the metal-plated door, I who know who I am, control what I do.

I have memory, I thought. I'm not one of those people who forget even their name. I remember. I remembered, in fact, the two men who had worked on the door, the older and the younger. Which of the two had said to me: pay attention, signora, pay attention not to force it, pay attention to how you use the keys, the mechanisms "ha ha" are delicate. They both had a sly look. All those allusions, the key in vertically, the key in horizontally, luckily I had always known my job. If after what Mario had done to me, after the outrage of abandonment preceded by that long period of deception, I was still I, persisting in the face of the turmoil of those months, here in the heat of early August, and was resisting, resisting so many disconnected adversities, this meant that what I had feared most since I was a child—to grow up and become like the *poverella*, that was the fear I had harbored for three decades—had not happened, I was reacting well, very well, I was holding tight around me the parts of my life, compliments, Olga, in spite of everything I wasn't leaving myself.

I stood for a while in front of the door, as if I really had been running. All right, I'll ask Carrano for help, even if he's the one who poisoned Otto. There's nothing else to do, I'll ask him if I can use his telephone. And if he wants to try to fuck me again, to do it in my ass, I'll say no, the moment has passed, I'm here only because there's an emergency in my house, don't get the wrong idea. I'll tell him that right away, so that it won't even occur to him that I've come to him for that sort of thing. When you miss your chance, there aren't any others. Maybe there's no second time without a third, but there is a first time without a second. Since that one time you came by yourself in the condom, you shit.

But I knew immediately, even before trying, that the door wouldn't open. And when I held the key and tried to turn it, the thing that I had predicted a minute before happened. The key wouldn't turn.

I was gripped by anxiety, precisely the wrong reaction. I applied more pressure, chaotically, I tried to turn the key first to the left, then to the right. No luck. Then I tried to take it out of the lock, but it wouldn't come out, it remained in the key-hole as if metal had fused to metal. I beat my fists against the panels, I pushed with my shoulder, I tried the key again, suddenly my body woke up, I was consumed by desperation. When I stopped, I discovered that I was covered with sweat. My nightgown was stuck to me, but my teeth were chattering. I felt cold, in spite of the heat of the day.

I squatted on the floor, I had to reason. The workers, yes, had told me that I had to be careful, the mechanism could break. But they had told me in that tone men have when they exaggerate in order to exaggerate their own indispensability. Sexual indispensability, above all. I remembered the sneer with which the older one had given me his card, in case I should need help. I knew perfectly well what lock he wished to intervene in, certainly not that of the reinforced door. Therefore, I said to myself, I had to eliminate from his words every real piece of information of a technical nature, he had used the jargon of his skills to suggest obscene things to me. Which meant, in practice, that I also had to eliminate from my head the alarming sense of those words, I didn't have to fear that the

mechanism of the door would jam. Good riddance to the
words of those two vulgar men, clean up. Relax the tension, re-
establish order, plug up the leaks in meaning. The dog, too, for
example: why should he have swallowed poison? Eliminate
"poison." I had seen Carrano close up—I felt like laughing at
the thought—and he didn't seem like a person who would prepare dog biscuits with strychnine, maybe Otto had only eaten
something rotten. Therefore preserve "rotten," stare hard at
the word. Reconsider every event of that day from the moment
of waking. Bring back Otto's spasms within the limits of prob-
ability, give back to the facts a sense of proportion. Give back
to me a sense of proportion. What was I? A woman worn out
by four months of tension and grief; not, surely, a witch who,
out of desperation, secretes a poison that can give a fever to her
male child, kill a domestic animal, put a telephone line out of
order, ruin the mechanism of a reinforced door lock. And
hurry up. The children hadn't eaten anything. I myself still had
to have breakfast, wash. The hours were passing. I had to separate the dark clothes from the white. I had no more clean
underwear. The vomit-stained sheets. Run the vacuum.
Housecleaning.

25.

I STOOD UP taking care not to make any abrupt movements. I
stared at the key for a long time, as if it were a mosquito to be
squashed, then I reached out my right hand decisively and
commanded the fingers to make the rotating movement to the
left. The key didn't move. I tried to pull it toward me, I hoped
it would shift just a tiny bit, just enough to find the right position, but I gained not a fraction of an inch. It didn't seem like

a key, it seemed an excrescence of the brass plate, a dark arch
in it.

I examined the panels. They were smooth, without knobs
apart from the glittering handle, massive on massive hinges.
Useless, there was no way to open the door except by turning
that key. I studied the round plates of the two locks, the key
was sticking out of the lower one. Each was fixed by four
screws of small dimensions. I already knew that to unscrew
them wouldn't get me very far, but I thought that doing it
would encourage me not to give up.

I went to the storage closet to get the tool box, I dragged it
to the front door. I dug around in it, but couldn't find a screw-
driver to fit those screws, all too big. So I went to the kitchen,
took a knife. I chose a screw at random and stuck the point of
the blade in the tiny crossed channel, but the knife jumped
away immediately, it got no purchase. I went back to the screw-
drivers, I took the smallest, I tried to slide the end under the
brass plate of the lower lock, another useless gesture. I gave up
after a few attempts and went back to the storage closet. I
searched slowly, careful not to lose my concentration, for a
strong object to insert under the door, that might serve as a
lever to raise one of the panels and pry it off its hinges. I rea-
soned, I must admit, as if I were telling myself a fable, without
in the least believing that I would find the right instrument, or
that, if I had found it, I would have the physical strength to do
what I had in mind. But I was fortunate, I found a short iron
bar that ended in a point. I went back to the entrance and tried
to insert the sharp end of the object under the door. There was
no room, the panels adhered perfectly to the floor, and besides,
even if I had succeeded—I realized—the space at the top
would be insufficient to allow the door to come off the hinges.
I let the bar fall and it made a loud noise. I didn't know what
else to try, I was an incompetent, a prisoner in my own house.

For the first time in the course of the day, I felt tears in my eyes, and I wasn't sorry.

26.

I WAS ABOUT TO CRY when Ilaria, who evidently had arrived on tiptoe behind me, asked:

"What are you doing?"

It was, of course, not a real question, she only wanted me to turn around and see her. I did, I felt a shudder of loathing. She had dressed in my clothes, she had put on makeup, she was wearing on her head an old blond wig that her father had given her. On her feet was a pair of my high-heeled shoes, on top a blue dress of mine that hampered her movements and made a long train behind her, her face was a painted mask, eye shadow, blush, lipstick. She looked to me like an old dwarf, one of those my mother used to tell of seeing in the funicular at Vomero when she was a girl. They were identical twins, a hundred years old, she said, who got on the cars and without saying a word began to play the mandolin. They had tow-colored hair, heavily shadowed eyes, wrinkled faces with red cheeks, painted lips. When they finished their concert, instead of saying thank you they stuck out their tongues. I had never seen them, but the stories of adults are thick with images, I had the two old dwarves clearly, vividly, in my mind. Now Ilaria was before me and she seemed to have come precisely from those stories of childhood.

When she became aware of the revulsion that must have showed on my face, the child smiled in embarrassment, and, eyes sparkling, said as if to justify herself:

"We're identical."

The sentence disturbed me, I shuddered, in a flash I lost that bit of ground I seemed to have gained. What did it mean, we are identical, at that moment I needed to be identical only to myself. I couldn't, I mustn't imagine myself as one of the old women of the funicular. At the mere idea I felt a slight dizziness, a veil of nausea. Everything began to break down again. Maybe, I thought, Ilaria herself wasn't Ilaria. Maybe she really was one of those minuscule women of The Vomero, who had appeared by surprise, just as, earlier, the *poverella* who had drowned herself at Capo Miseno had. Or maybe not. Maybe for a long time I had been one of those old mandolin players, and Mario had discovered it and had left me. Without realizing it, I had been transformed into one of them, a figure of childish fantasies, and now Ilaria was only returning to me my true image, she had tried to resemble me by making herself up like me. This was the reality that I was about to discover, behind the appearance of so many years. I was already no longer I, I was someone else, as I had feared since waking up, as I had feared since who knows when. Now any resistance was useless, I was lost just as I was laboring with all my strength not to lose myself, I was no longer there, at the entrance to my house, in front of the reinforced door, coming to grips with that disobedient key. I was only pretending to be there, as in a child's game.

Making an effort, I seized Ilaria by the hand and dragged her along the hall. She protested, but feebly, she lost a shoe, she wriggled free, she lost the wig, she said:

"You're mean, I can't stand you."

I opened the door of the bathroom and, avoiding the mirror, dragged the child over to the bathtub that was full to the brim. With one hand I held Ilaria by the head and immersed her in the water, while with the other I rubbed her face energetically. Reality, reality, without rouge. I needed this, for now, if I wanted to save myself, save my children, the dog. To insist, that is, on assigning myself the job of savior. There, washed. I pulled the child out and she sprayed water in my face, blowing and writhing and gasping for breath and crying:

"You made me drink it, you were drowning me."

I said to her with sudden tenderness, again I felt like crying:

"I wanted to see how pretty my Ilaria is, I had forgotten how pretty she is."

I scooped up water in the hollow of my hand and then, as she wriggled and tried to get free, began again to rub her face, her lips, her eyes, mixing the remaining colors, loosening them and pasting them on her skin, until she became a doll with a purple face.

"There you are," I said, trying to embrace her, "that's how I like you."

She pushed me away, she cried:

"Go away! Why can you wear makeup and I can't?"

"You're right, I shouldn't, either."

I left her and immersed my face, my hair in the cold water. I felt better. When I stood up and rubbed the skin of my face with both hands, I felt under my fingers the wet cotton that I had in one nostril and I took it out cautiously and threw it in the tub. The cotton floated, black with blood.

"Is it better now?"

"We were prettier before."

"We are pretty if we love each other."

"You don't love me, you hurt my wrist."

"I love you very much."

"Not me."

"Really?"

"No."

"Then if you love me, you have to help me."

"What do I have to do?"

A flash, a throb in the wrists, the abrupt skid of things, I turned uncertainly to the mirror again. I wasn't in a good state: my hair wet and stuck to my forehead, one nostril encrusted with blood, the makeup faded or reduced to small black clots, the lipstick washed off my lips but smeared around my nose and chin. I reached out a hand to take a cotton ball.

"Well?" Ilaria pressed me, impatiently.

The voice reached me from far away. Just a moment. First take off the makeup for good. Thanks to the side panels of the mirror, I saw the two halves of my face separately, far apart, and I was drawn first by my right profile, then by the left. They were both completely unfamiliar to me, normally I didn't use the side panels, I recognized myself only in the image reflected by the big mirror. Now I tried to arrange the mirrors so that I could see from the side and from the front. There is no technical means of reproduction that, up to now, has managed to surpass the mirror and the dream. Look at me, I said to the glass in a whisper, a breath. The mirror was summing up my situation. If the frontal image reassured me, saying to me that I was Olga and that perhaps I would arrive at the end of the day successfully, my two profiles warned me that it was not so. They showed me my neck, the ugly living ears, the lightly arched nose that I had never liked, the chin, the high cheekbones and the taut skin of the cheeks, like a white page. I felt that there, over those two half portions, Olga had scant control, she was not very resistant, not very persistent. What did she have to do with those images. The worse side, the better side, geometry of the hidden. If I had lived in the belief that I was the frontal Olga, others had always attributed to me the shifting, uncertain welding of the two profiles, an inclusive image that I knew nothing about. To Mario, to Mario above all, I thought I had given Olga, the Olga of the central mirror, and now, in reality, I didn't know which face, which body I had given him. He had assembled me on the basis of those two shifting, disjointed, ephemeral sides, and I don't know what physiognomy he had attributed to me, what montage of me had made him fall in love, what, on the other hand, had turned out to be repugnant to him, making him fall out of love. For Mario I—I shuddered—had never been Olga. The meanings, the meaning of her life—I suddenly understood—were only a dazzlement of late adolescence, my illusion of stability. Starting now, if I wanted to make it, I had to trust myself to those two profiles, to their strangeness rather than to their familiarity, and moving on from there very slowly restore confidence in myself, make myself adult.

That conclusion seemed to me very true. Especially since, looking hard into my half face on the left, at the changing physiognomy of the secret sides, I recognized the features of the *poverella*—never would I have imagined that we had so many elements in common. Her profile, when she descended the stairs and interrupted my games and those of my companions to pass by with her absent gaze of suffering, had been huddling in me for years, it was that which I now offered to the mirror. The woman murmured to me from the panel:

"Remember that the dog is dying and Gianni has a nasty intestinal fever."

"Thank you," I said without fear, in fact with gratitude.

"Thank you for what?" asked Ilaria, annoyed.

I shook myself.

"Thank you for having promised that you would help me."

"But you haven't told me what I have to do!"

I smiled, I said:

"Come with me and I'll show you."

27.

I MOVED, I SEEMED TO MYSELF to be pure air compressed between the poorly connected halves of a single figure. How inconclusive it was to traverse that known house. All its spaces had been transformed into separate platforms, far away from one another. Once, five years earlier, I had known its dimensions minutely, I had measured every corner, I had furnished it with care. Now I didn't know how far the bathroom was from the living room, the living room from the storage closet, the storage closet from the front hall. I was pulled here and there, as if in a game, I had a sense of vertigo.

"Mamma, watch out," said Ilaria and grabbed my hand. I staggered, perhaps I was about to fall. At the entrance, I pointed out to her the toolbox.

"Take the hammer," I said, "and follow me."

We went back, now she held the hammer proudly in both hands, she seemed finally happy that I was her mother. And I, too, was pleased. Once in the living room I said to her:

"Now sit here and bang on the floor without stopping."

Ilaria took on an expression of great amusement.

"That's going to make Signor Carrano angry."

"Exactly."

"And if he comes up to complain?"

"Call me and I'll speak to him."

The child went to the middle of the room and began to beat the floor, holding the hammer in both hands.

Now, I thought, I must see how Gianni is, I'm forgetting about him, what a careless mother.

I exchanged a final glance of understanding with Ilaria and started to go, but my eyes fell on an object that was lying out of place, at the foot of the bookcase. It was the spray can of insecticide, it should have been in the storage closet, instead it was there on the floor, dented by Otto's jaws, even the white spray top had come off.

I picked it up, examined it, looked around disoriented, noticed the ants. They ran in a line along the base of the book-case, they had returned to besiege the house, perhaps they were the only black thread that held it together, that kept it from dis-integrating completely. Without their obstinacy, I thought, Ilaria would now be on a splinter of floor much farther away than she seems and the room where Gianni is lying would be harder to reach than a castle whose drawbridge has been raised, and the room of pain where Otto is in agony would be a leper colony, and impenetrable, and my very emotions and thoughts and memories of the past, foreign places and the city of my birth and the table under which I listened to my mother's sto-ries, would be a speck of dust in the burning light of August. Leave the ants in peace. Maybe they weren't an enemy, I had been wrong to try to exterminate them. At times the solidity of things is entrusted to irritating elements that appear to disrupt their cohesion.

This last thought had a loud voice, it echoed, I started, it wasn't mine. I heard its sound clearly, it had even managed to penetrate the barrier of Ilaria's diligent blows. I looked up from the spray can I had in my hands to my desk. The papier-mâché body of the poor woman of Naples was sitting there, an arti-san's soldering of my two profiles. She was keeping herself alive with my veins, I saw them red, uncovered, wet, pulsing. Even the throat, the vocal chords, even the breath to make them vibrate belonged to me. After uttering those incongruous words, she went back to writing in my notebook.

Although I stayed where I was, I was able to see what she was writing. Her own notes, in my pages. This room is too big, she wrote in my handwriting, I can't concentrate, I can't com-pletely understand where I am, what I'm doing, why. The night

is long, it won't end, therefore my husband left me, he wanted
nights that raced, before getting old, dying. In order to write
well, I need to go to the heart of every question, of a smaller,
safer place. Eliminate the superfluous. Narrow the field. To
write truly is to speak from the depths of the maternal womb.
Turn the page, Olga, begin again from the beginning.

I didn't sleep last night, the woman at the desk said to me.
But I remembered going to bed. I slept a little, I got up, I went
back to sleep. I must have thrown myself on the bed very late,
cutting across it diagonally, that's why, upon waking, I'd found
myself in that anomalous position.

Pay attention, though, reorder the facts. Already in the
course of the night something inside me had yielded and broken. Reason and memory had flaked off, sorrow that lasts too
long is capable of this. I had believed I was going to bed and
yet I had not. Or I had and then had got up. Disobedient body.
It wrote in my notebooks, wrote pages and pages. It wrote with
the left hand, to fight fear, to hold off humiliation. Probably it
had happened like that.

I felt the weight of the spray can, maybe I had struggled all
night with the ants, in vain. I had sprayed insecticide in every
room of the house and that was why Otto was sick, why Gianni
had vomited so much. Or maybe not. My opaque sides were
inventing culpability that Olga didn't have. Painting me careless, irresponsible, incompetent, leading me to a self-denigration that would later confuse the real situation and keep me
from marking its margins, establish what was, what was not.

I placed the spray can on a shelf, backed up toward the door
on tiptoe, as if I didn't want to disturb the outline of the
woman at the desk who had started writing again, Ilaria who
was continuing to pound methodically. I headed again to the
bathroom, fighting the fantasies of guilt. Poor boy, my fragile
male child. I looked for the Novalgina in the disarray of the

medicine cabinet and when I found it I poured twelve drops (twelve, precise) in a glass of water. Was it possible that I could have been so negligent? Possible that I had sprayed insecticide during the night, using up the contents of the can, with the windows closed?

In the hall I heard Gianni retching. I found him leaning over the side of the bed, his eyes staring, his face flushed, his mouth open, while a force shook him from within, in vain. Luckily I could no longer contain anything, a feeling, an emotion, a suspicion. Again the picture was changing, other facts, other probabilities. I thought of the cannon in front of the Cittadella. What if, climbing inside the old gun, Gianni had breathed in a malady of miseries and distant climes, a sign of the world at the boiling point, everything in flux, borders fluid, the far that becomes near, rumors of subversion, old and new hatreds, wars distant or at the gates? I yielded to all fantasies, all terrors. The universe of good reasons that I had been given after adolescence was narrowing. No matter how much I had tried to be slow, to have thoughtful gestures, that world over the years had nevertheless moved in too great a whirl, and its globelike figure was reduced to a thin round tablet, so thin that, as fragments splintered off, it appeared to be pierced in the middle, soon it would become like a wedding ring, finally it would dissolve.

I sat beside Gianni, I held his head, I encouraged him to throw up. Exhausted, he spit out a greenish saliva, and finally fell back, crying.

"I called you and you didn't come," he rebuked me through his tears.

I dried his mouth, his eyes. I had been forced to deal with certain problems, I justified myself, I had to sort them out urgently, I hadn't heard him.

"Is it true that Otto ate poison?"

"No, it's not true."

"Ilaria told me he did."

"Ilaria is full of nonsense."

"I hurt here," he sighed, showing me his neck. "It hurts a lot, but I don't want to have a suppository."

"I'm not going to give you one, just take these drops."

"They'll make me throw up again."

"With the drops you won't throw up."

He struggled to drink the water, he retched, he fell back on the pillow. I felt his forehead, it was burning. His dry skin seemed to me unbearable, hot as a cake that's just come out of the oven. Ilaria's hammering, too, seemed to me unbearable, even at a distance. They were energetic blows, they resounded throughout the house.

"What's that?" asked Gianni, frightened.

"The neighbor is doing some work."

"It's bothering me, tell him to stop."

"All right," I reassured him and then I made him hold the thermometer. He agreed only because I hugged him hard with both arms and held him against me.

"My child," I sang softly, rocking him. "My sick child who's now getting better."

In a few minutes, in spite of Ilaria's persistent hammering, Gianni fell asleep, but his eyelids wouldn't close completely, there was a rosy edge, a whitish thread between the lashes. I waited a little, anxious about his too heavy breathing and the mobility of the pupils that could be sensed under the eyelids; then I took out the thermometer. The mercury had gone up, to almost a hundred and four.

I placed the thermometer on the night table in disgust, as if it were alive. I laid Gianni on the sheet, on the pillow, staring at the red hole of his mouth, hanging open as if he were dead. Ilaria's blows hammered in my brain. Return to myself, rectify the misdeed of the night, of the day. They're my children, I thought, to convince myself, my creatures. Even if Mario had made them with some woman he had imagined; even if I, however, believed that I was Olga making them with him; even if now my husband attributed meaning and value only to a girl named Carla, another blunder of his, and didn't recognize in me the body, the physiology that he had attributed to me in order to love me, inseminate me; even if I myself had never been that woman or—I now knew—the Olga I had thought I was; even if, oh God, I was only a disjointed composition of sides, a forest of cubist figures unfamiliar even to myself, those creatures were mine, my true creatures born from my body, this body, I was responsible for them.

Therefore, with an effort that cost me a struggle to the limit of the bearable, I got to my feet. I have to take hold of myself, understand. Get back in touch immediately.

28.

WHERE HAD I PUT the cell phone? The day I had broken it, where had I put the pieces? I went to the bedroom, rummaged through the drawer of my night table, it was there, two purple halves, separated.

Probably just because I knew nothing about the mechanics of a cell phone, I wanted to convince myself that it wasn't broken at all. I examined the half that had the display and the keypad, I pressed the button that turned it on, nothing happened. Maybe, I said to myself, I only have to stick the two parts together to make it work. I played around for a while, randomly. I put in the battery, which had come out, I tried to make the pieces fit together. I discovered that they slipped apart from each other because the central body was broken, the channel for the joint had splintered. We fabricate objects in a semblance of our bodies, one side joined to the other. Or we design them thinking they're joined as we are joined to the desired body. Creatures born from a banal fantasy. Mario—it suddenly seemed to me—in spite of success in his work, in spite of his skills and his lively intelligence, was a man of banal fantasy. Maybe for that very reason he would have known how to make the cell phone function again. And so he would have saved the dog, the child. Success depends on the capacity to manipulate the obvious with calculated precision. I didn't know how to adapt, I didn't know how to yield completely to Mario's gaze. I had tried. Obtuse though I was, I pretended to be a right angle, and had managed to choke off even my vocation of moving from fantasy to fantasy. It hadn't been sufficient, he had withdrawn anyway, he had gone to be joined more solidly elsewhere.

No, stop it. Think of the cell phone. In the drawer I found a green ribbon, I tied the two halves tightly together and tried to press the on button. Nothing. I hoped for a sort of magic, I tried to hear a dial tone. Nothing, nothing, nothing.

I abandoned the instrument on the bed, worn out by Ilaria's hammering. Then in a flash the computer came to mind. How had I not thought of it. A fault of how I was made, I knew so little, the final proof. I went to the living room, moving as if the hammer blows were a gray curtain, a curtain through which I had to open a way for myself with arms outstretched, hands groping.

I found the child crouching on the floor and banging the hammer, just as she had been. The pounding was insupportable, I counted on its being that way also for Carrano.

"Can I stop?" she asked, all sweaty, red in the face, eyes shining.

"No, it's important, keep going."

"You do it, I'm tired."

"I have something else urgent to do."

At my desk now there was no one. I sat down, the seat conserved no human warmth. I turned on the computer, I went to the mail icon, I typed to send or receive e-mail. I hoped to succeed in connecting in spite of the disturbance that kept me from telephoning, I hoped that the problem was limited to the instrument, as the person at the telephone company had said. I thought of sending requests for help to all the friends and acquaintances who showed up among my and Mario's contacts. But the computer tried over and over again without success to make a connection. It searched for the line with prolonged sounds of discomfort, it snorted, it gave up. I clutched the edges of the keyboard, I rotated my gaze over here, over there in order not to feel anxiety, occasionally my eyes fell on the still open notebook, on the sentences underlined in red: "Where am I? What am I doing? Why?" Anna's words, stupidly motivated by the suspicion that her lover is about to betray her, leave her. Such tensions without sense push us to formulate questions of meaning. For a moment Ilaria's hammering sliced the anxious thread of sounds emitted by the computer as if an eel had slid through the room and the child were chopping it in pieces. I resisted as long as I could, then I shouted.

"That's enough! Stop that hammering!"

Ilaria, opening her mouth wide in surprise, stopped.

"I told you I wanted to stop."

I nodded yes, depressed. I had yielded, Carrano hadn't. From no corner of the building had a single sign of life been roused. I was acting without a plan, I couldn't stick with one strategy. The only ally I had in the world was that child of seven and I constantly risked ruining my relations with her.

I looked at the computer screen, nothing. I got up and went to embrace the child, I emitted a long groan.

"Do you have a headache?" she asked me.

"It will pass," I answered.

"Shall I massage your temples?"

"Yes."

I sat on the floor while Ilaria carefully rubbed my temples with her fingers. Here I was, giving in again, how much time did I think I had available, Gianni, Otto.

"I'll make everything go away," she said. "Do you feel better?"

I nodded yes.

"Why did you put that clip on your arm?"

I roused myself, saw the clip, I had forgotten it. The tiny pain it caused me had become a constitutional part of my flesh. Useless, that is. I took it off, I left it on the floor.

"It helps me remember. Today is a day when everything is slipping my mind, I don't know what to do."

"I'll help you."

"Really?"

I got up, took from the desk a metal paper cutter.

"Hold this," I said to her, "and if you see me getting distracted, poke me."

The child took the paper cutter and observed me attentively.

"How will I know if you're distracted?"

"You can tell. A distracted person is a person who no longer smells odors, doesn't hear words, doesn't feel anything."

She showed me the paper cutter.

"And if you don't even feel this?"

"Prick me until I feel it. Now come on."

29.

I DRAGGED HER BEHIND ME to the storage closet. I rooted around everywhere in search of a strong rope, I was sure I had one. Instead I found only a ball of string for tying packages. I went to the entrance hall, I tied one end of the string to the short iron bar that I had left on the floor, in front of the armored door. Followed by Ilaria, I returned to the living room, went out onto the balcony.

I collided with a gust of warm wind that had just bowed the trees, leaving behind an irritating rustle of leaves. I almost lost my breath, the short nightgown stuck to my body, Ilaria was grabbing the hem with her free hand, as if she were afraid of flying away. In the air was a thick smell of wild mint, of dust, of bark burned by the sun.

I leaned over the balcony, I tried to look onto the balcony below, which belonged to Carrano.

"Don't fall," Ilaria said to me in alarm, holding on to my nightgown.

The window was closed, the only sound was the song of some birds, the distant rumble of a bus. No human voices. On all five floors, below, to the right, to the left, I couldn't make out a sign of life. I strained to hear the music from a radio, a song, the chatter of a television show. Nothing, nothing nearby, at least, nothing that was indistinguishable from the periodic roar of leaves stirred by that incongruous burning wind. I shouted over and over, in a weak voice, a voice that, in any case, had never had great power:

"Carrano! Aldo! Is anyone there? Help! Help me."

Nothing happened, the wind cut the words off my lips as if I were trying to speak while bringing a cup of boiling liquid to my mouth.

Ilaria, now visibly tense, asked:

"Why do we need help?"

I didn't answer, I didn't know what to say, I mumbled:

"Don't worry, we'll help ourselves."

I stuck the bar through the railing, I let out the string, dropping the bar until it touched Carrano's railing. I leaned over to try to see how far it was from the window and immediately Ilaria let go of my nightgown and held tight instead to a bare leg, I felt her breathing against my skin, saying:

"I'll hold you, mamma."

I stretched my right arm down as far as possible, I gripped the string tight between thumb and forefinger, then I gave a swinging motion to the bar with rapid, decisive pulses. The bar—I saw—began to move like a pendulum along Carrano's balcony. In order for the motion to be successful, I leaned my chest out farther and farther, I stared at the bar as if I wanted to hypnotize myself, I watched that dark pointed segment, now flying above the pavement, now coming back to graze my neighbor's railing. I soon lost the fear of falling, it seemed to me in fact that my balcony was no farther from the street than the length of the string. I wanted to hit Carrano's windows. I wanted the bar to break them and penetrate his house, the living room where he had received me the night before. I felt like laughing. Surely he was lazing in bed, in a half sleep, a man on the threshold of physical decay, a man of dubious erections, a casual lover unfit for reascending the slope of humiliation. Imagining how he spent the days, I felt an impulse of contempt for him. In the hottest hours of the day he would take a long siesta in the half-light, sweating, his breath heavy, waiting to go and play in some faded orchestra, with no more hope. I recalled his rough tongue, the salty taste of his mouth, and I came to only when I felt the point of Ilaria's paper cutter against the skin of my right thigh. Good girl: attentive, sensible. That was the tactile signal I needed. I let the string run through my fingers, the bar disappeared at great speed under the floor of my balcony. I heard the sound of broken glass, the string broke, I saw the bar tumble along the tiles of the balcony below, bump the railing, and fall into the void. It fell for a long time, followed by sparkling fragments of glass, hitting from floor to floor the railings of other balconies, all the same, a black bar, smaller and smaller. It landed on the pavement, ricocheting several times with a distant ringing.

I drew back, frightened, the abyss of the fifth floor had regained its depth. I felt Ilaria tight on my leg. I waited for the hoarse voice of the musician, anger at the damage I had caused. There was no reaction. Instead the birds returned, the wave of burning wind that hit me and the child, my daughter, a true invention of my flesh that forced me to reality.

"You did well," I said.

"If I hadn't held you, you would have fallen."

"You don't hear anything?"

"No."

"Then let's call: Carrano, Carrano, help!"

We shouted together, for a long time, but still Carrano gave no sign of life. There answered instead a long feeble bark, it might be from a distant dog, abandoned in the summer on the side of the road, or Otto himself.

30.

GET MOVING AGAIN, right away, think of solutions. Avoid surrendering to the senselessness of the day, hold the fragments of life together as if they still had their allotted place in a design. I nodded to Ilaria to follow me, I smiled at her. Now she was the lady of the sword, she held in her hand the paper cutter, she had taken her task so seriously that her knuckles were white.

Where I had failed, maybe she would succeed, I thought. We went back to the entrance, in front of the door.

"Try to turn the key," I asked her.

Ilaria switched the paper cutter from her right hand to her left, stretched out her arm, she couldn't reach the key. So I held her around the waist, lifted her up as high as necessary.

"Do I turn here?" she asked.

"No, on the other side."

Tender little hand, fingers of vapor. She tried and tried again, but didn't have the strength. She couldn't have done it even if the key hadn't been jammed.

I put her down, she was disappointed that she hadn't proved herself up to the new task I had entrusted to her. In a sudden shift she became angry with me.

"Why are you making me do something that you should do yourself?" she said reproachfully.

"Because you're better."

"You don't know how to open the door anymore?" She was alarmed.

"No."

"Like that other time?"

I looked at her uncertainly.

"What time?"

"The time we went to the country."

I felt a sharp, protracted pain in my chest. How could she remember, she couldn't have been more than three.

"Sometimes with keys you're really stupid and it's embarrassing," she added, to make it clear to me that she remembered very well.

I shook my head. No, in general with keys I had a good relationship. Usually I opened doors with a natural gesture, I didn't feel any anxiety that a lock might jam. Sometimes, however, especially with unknown locks—a hotel room, for example—I immediately got confused and although I was embarrassed went back to the reception desk; it could happen especially if the key was electronic. Those magnetic cards made me anxious, a hint of a thought was enough, the sense of a possible difficulty, and the gesture lost naturalness, I was no longer able to open the door.

The hands forgot, the fingers had no memory of the right grip, the correct pressure. Like that other time. How humiliated I had been. Gina, the mother of the little traitor Carla, had given me the keys to their country house so that I could go there with the children. I had left, Mario had things to do, he would join us the following day. In the late afternoon, after a couple of hours in the car, unnerved by the fierce weekend traffic, by the children, who had quarreled continuously, by Otto, still a puppy, whimpering, I had arrived at the house. I had spent the whole trip thinking about how I was stupidly wasting time, I couldn't read, I was no longer writing, I had no social role that provided encounters, conflicts, sympathies. The woman I as an adolescent had imagined I would be, what had become of her? I envied Gina, who at the time worked with Mario. They always had things to discuss, my husband talked more to her than to me. And already Carla had begun to annoy me, she seemed so certain of her destiny, and at times even ventured some criticism, said I was too devoted to the children, to the house, she praised my first book, she exclaimed: if I were you, I would think above all of my work. Not only was she beautiful but she had been brought up by her mother in the secure prospect of a bright future. It seemed to her natural to interfere in everything, even though she was only fifteen, she often wanted to teach me something and would spout opinions on things she knew nothing about. Her voice alone by then could put me on edge.

I had parked in the courtyard, but was agitated by my thoughts. What was I doing there with two children and a puppy. I had gone to the door and tried to open it. But I hadn't succeeded, and no matter how I tried and tried again—

meanwhile it was growing dark, Gianni and Ilaria, tired and hungry, were whining—I couldn't do it. Yet I didn't want to telephone Mario, out of pride, out of arrogance, out of not wanting to make him come to my rescue after a hard day at work. The children and little Otto ate some cookies, they fell asleep in the car. I went back and tried again, I had tried again and again, my fingers worn out, stiff, until I gave up, I had sat on a step and let the weight of the night fall on me.

At ten in the morning Mario arrived. But not alone. With him, unexpectedly, were the owners of the house. What happened, what in the world, why didn't you telephone. I explained, stammering, furious because my husband, ill at ease, joked about my incompetence, painting me as a woman of great imagination but useless in practical matters, an idiot, in short. There had been—I recall—a long look between me and Carla, which had seemed to me a look of complicity, of understanding, as if she wished to say to me: rebel, say how things are, say that you're the one who confronts practical life every day, the obligations, the burden of the children. That look had surprised me, but evidently I had not understood its true significance. Or perhaps I had understood it, it was the look of a girl who was wondering how she would have treated that seductive man, if she had been in my place. Gina meanwhile had put the key in the lock and opened the door without any problem.

I shook myself, I felt the point of the paper cutter on the skin of my left arm.

"You're distracted," said Ilaria.

"No, I was just thinking that you're right."

"Right about what?"

"Right. Why couldn't I open the door that time?"

"I told you, because sometimes you're stupid."

"Yes."

31.

YES, I WAS STUPID. The channels of my senses were blocked, how long had it been since life flowed in them. What a mistake it had been to close off the meaning of my existence in the rites that Mario offered with cautious conjugal rapture. What a mistake it had been to entrust the sense of myself to his gratifications, his enthusiasms, to the ever more productive course of his life. What a mistake, above all, it had been to believe that I couldn't live without him, when for a long time I had not been at all certain that I was alive with him. Where was his skin under my fingers, for example, where was the heat of his mouth. If I were to interrogate myself deeply—and I had always avoided doing it—I would have to admit that my body, in recent years, had been truly receptive, truly welcoming, only on obscure occasions, pure chance: the pleasure of seeing, and seeing again, a casual acquaintance who had paid attention to me, had praised my intelligence, my talent, had touched my hand with admiration; a tremor of happiness at an unexpected encounter in the street, with someone I had worked with in the past; the verbal fencing, or silences, with a friend of Mario's who had let me understand that he would like to be my friend in particular, the enjoyment in certain attentions of ambiguous meaning addressed to me at various times, maybe yes maybe no, more yes than no if only I had been willing, if I had dialed a telephone number with the right excuse at the right moment, it happens it doesn't happen, the palpitation of events with unpredictable outcomes.

Maybe I should have started there, at the point when Mario told me that he wanted to leave me. I should have moved from the fact that the captivating figure of a man who was practically a stranger, a random man—a "perhaps" that had to be untangled but would in the end be rewarding—was capable of giving meaning, let's say, to a fleeting odor of gasoline, the gray trunk of a city plane tree, and to fix forever in that chance place of meeting an intense feeling of joy, an expectation; while nothing, nothing of Mario possessed the same earth-quake-like movement anymore, and every gesture had only the power to be put in the right place, in the same secure net, without deviations, without excesses. If I were to start from there, from those secret emotions, perhaps I would understand better why he had gone and why I, who had always set against the occasional emotional confusion the stable order of our affections, now felt so violently the bitterness of loss, an intolerable grief, the anxiety of falling out of the web of certainties and having to relearn life without the security of knowing how to do it.

Relearning how to turn a key, for example. Was it possible that Mario, leaving, had taken from my hands that ability? Was it possible that he had begun already, that morning in the country, when his happy abandonment of himself to two strangers had lacerated me inside, to rip from my fingers their ability to grip? Was it possible that the imbalance and the pain had begun then, while he tested, right before my eyes, the happiness of seduction, and I recognized in his face a pleasure that I had often touched but had always suspended for fear of destroying the guarantees of our relationship?

Punctually Ilaria pricked me, several times, I think, painfully, for I reacted with a start and she drew back exclaiming:

"You told me to do it!"

I nodded yes, I reassured her with a gesture, with the other hand I rubbed the ankle where she had struck me. I tried again to open the door, I couldn't do it. I leaned over, I examined the key closely. Finding the imprint of the old gestures was a mistake. I had to disengage them. Under the stupefied gaze of Ilaria, I brought my mouth to the key, tasted it with my lips, smelled its odor of plastic and metal. Then I grabbed it solidly between my teeth and tried to make it turn. I did it with a sudden jerk, as if I wished to surprise the object, impose a new statute, a different dispensation. Now we'll see who wins, I thought, while a pasty, salty taste invaded my mouth. But I produced no effect, except the impression that, because the rotating movement of my teeth on the key wasn't working, it was finding an outlet in my face, tearing it like a can opener, and my teeth were moving, were being unhinged from the foundation of my face, taking with them the nasal septum, an eyebrow, an eye, and revealing the viscid interior of head and throat.

I immediately pulled my mouth away from the key, it seemed to me that my face was hanging to one side like the coiled skin of an orange after the knife has begun to peel it. What is there still to try. Lie on my back, feel the cold floor against it. Stretch my bare legs against the panels of the door, clasp the soles of my feet around the key, fit its hostile beak between my heels to try again to capture the necessary movement. Yes, no, yes. For a while I let myself sink into desperation, which would mold me thoroughly, make me metal, door panel, mechanism, like an artist who works directly on his body. Then I noticed on my left thigh, above the knee, a painful gash. A cry escaped me, I realized that Ilaria had made a deep wound.

32.

I SAW HER BACK OFF in fear with the paper cutter in her right hand.

"Are you crazy?" I said, turning on her fiercely.

"You aren't listening to me," Ilaria cried. "I'm calling you and you can't hear me, you're doing terrible things, your eyes are all twisted, I'm going to tell daddy."

I looked at the cut above my knee, the strip of blood. I tore the paper cutter away from her. I threw it toward the open door of the storage closet.

"That's enough of that game," I said to her. "You don't know how to play. Now stay here and be good, don't move. We're locked in, we're prisoners, and your father will never come to save us. Look what you've done to me."

"You deserve worse," she retorted, her eyes bright with tears.

I tried to calm myself, I took a deep breath.

"Now don't start crying, don't you dare start crying…"

I didn't know what to say, what else to do, at that point. It seemed to me that I had tried everything, there was nothing left to do but restore clear outlines to the situation and accept it.

Displaying a false capacity to give orders, I said:

"We have two patients, Gianni and Otto. Now you, without crying, go and see how your brother is, I will go and see how Otto is."

"I have to stay with you and prick you, you told me to."

"I was wrong, Gianni is alone, he needs someone to feel his forehead, and put the refreshing coins on it, I can't do everything."

I pushed her toward the living room, she rebelled:

"Who's going to prick you if you get distracted?"

I looked at the long cut on my leg, from which a thick stripe of blood continued to well up.

"Call me every so often, and don't forget. That will be enough to keep me from being distracted."

She thought for a moment, then said:

"But hurry up, I get bored with Gianni, he doesn't know how to play."

That last phrase pained me. With that explicit reminder of

the game I realized that Ilaria didn't want to play anymore, that she was beginning to be seriously worried about me. If I had the responsibility for two sick creatures, she was starting to perceive that the sick who burdened her were three. Poor, poor little thing. She felt alone, she was secretly waiting for a father who wasn't showing up, she could no longer hold the confusion of that day within the limits of a game. I was now aware of her anguish, I added it to mine. How changeable it all is, nothing has fixed points. With every step I took toward Gianni's room, toward Otto's, I was afraid of feeling ill, of presenting to her I don't know what spectacle of collapse. I had to maintain judgment and the clarity of memory, they always go together, a binomial of health.

I pushed the little girl into the room, I glanced at the boy who was still sleeping and I went out, locking the door with a clear gesture, entirely natural. Although Ilaria protested, called me, beat her hands against the door, I ignored her and went to the room where Otto was lying. I didn't know what was happening to the dog. Ilaria loved him deeply, I didn't want her to be present at horrifying scenes. Protect her, yes, the truth of this preoccupation did me good. That the cold plan of guarding my children should slowly be transformed into an inescapable need, the principal preoccupation, seemed to me a positive sign.

In the dog's room, under Mario's desk, there was now the evil odor of death. I went in cautiously, Otto was still, he hadn't moved an inch. I crouched beside him, then sat on the floor.

First of all I saw the ants, they had arrived, they were exploring the muddy territory that lapped the dog's back. Otto, however, didn't care. It was as if he had turned gray, an island drained of color breathing its last. His muzzle, with the greenish saliva from the jaws, seemed to have corroded the material of the tiles and to be sinking into them. His eyes were closed.

"Forgive me," I said.

I ran the palm of my hand over the fur on his neck, he gave a jolt, his jaws unlocked, he emitted a threatening growl. I wanted to be forgiven for what I had perhaps done to him, for what I had been unable to do. I pulled him toward me, I rested his head on my legs. He gave off a sick heat that entered my blood. He barely moved his ears, his tail. I thought it was a sign of well-being, even his breath seemed less labored. The big spots of shining drool that were spreading like an enamel around the black edge of his mouth appeared to freeze, as if he had no longer any need to produce those humors of suffering.

How unbearable the body of a living being who fights with death, and now seems to win, now to lose. I don't know how long we remained like that. At times the dog's breathing accelerated as when he was healthy and was eager for a game, for a run in the open air, for understanding and petting, at times it became imperceptible. Even his body alternated moments of trembling and spasms with moments of absolute immobility. I felt the remains of his power slowly slip away, images of the past dripping out: the flight among the bright corpuscles of pressurized water from the sprinklers in the park, the inquisitive scratching among the bushes, the way he followed me through the house when he expected me to feed him. That proximity of real death, that bleeding wound of his suffering, of guilt, unexpectedly made me ashamed of my grief of the previous months, of that day with its overtones of unreality. I felt the room return to order, the house weld together its spaces, the solidity of the floor, the hot day that extended over everything, a transparent glue.

How could I have let myself go like that, let my senses disintegrate, the sense of being alive. I caressed Otto between the ears and he opened his colorless eyes and stared at me. I saw in him the look of the friendly dog who, instead of accusing me, asked forgiveness for his condition. Then an intense pain in his body obscured his pupils, he gnashed his teeth and barked at me without ferocity. Soon afterward he died in my lap, and I burst out crying in an uncontrollable lament, utterly unlike any other crying of those days, those months.

When my eyes dried and the last sobs died in my breast, I realized that Mario had become again the good man he had perhaps always been, I no longer loved him.

33.

I LAID THE DOG'S head on the floor, I got up. Slowly the voice of Ilaria returned, calling me, immediately afterward Gianni's joined it. I looked around, I saw the feces black with blood, the ants, the dead body. I went out of the room, I went to get a bucket, a rag. I opened the windows, cleaned the room, working quickly but efficiently. I kept calling to the children:

"Just a minute, I'm coming."

It seemed to me brutal that Otto was lying there, I didn't want the children to see him. I tried to pick him up, I didn't have the strength. I took him by the back paws and dragged him across the floor to the living room, onto the balcony. How heavy a body that has been traversed by death is, life is light, there's no need to let anyone make it heavy for us. I looked for a moment at the dog's fur ruffled by the wind, then I went back in and, despite the heat, closed the window carefully.

The house was silent, it now seemed to me small, concentrated, without dark corners, made almost cheerful by the voices of the children who, laughing, had begun to make a game of calling me. Ilaria said mamma with the voice of a soprano, Gianni repeated mamma like a tenor.

I hurried to them, I opened the door with a secure motion, I said gaily:

"Here's mamma."

Ilaria threw herself on me, hit me again and again, slapping my legs.

"You mustn't lock me in."

"It's true, I'm sorry. But I unlocked you."

I sat on Gianni's bed, he was certainly less feverish, he seemed like a boy who couldn't wait to go back to playing with his sister, to shouting, laughing, furiously quarreling. I felt his forehead, the drops had had an effect, his skin was warm, just slightly sweaty.

"Does your head still hurt?"

"No. I'm hungry."

"I'll make you some rice."

"I don't like rice."

"I don't, either," Ilaria added.

"The rice I make is very good."

"Where's Otto?" asked Gianni.

I hesitated.

"In there, he's sleeping, leave him alone."

And I was about to say something else, about the dog's serious illness, something that would prepare them for his disappearance from their life, when, completely unexpectedly, we heard the electric charge of the doorbell.

All three of us were as if suspended, without moving.

"Daddy," murmured Ilaria, full of hope.

I said:

"I don't think so, it's not daddy. Wait here, I forbid you to move, you're in big trouble if you leave this room. I'm going to open the door."

They recognized my normal tone, firm but also ironic, words deliberately excessive for minimal situations. I recognized it myself, I accepted it, they accepted it.

I went along the hall, reached the entrance. Was it possible that Mario had remembered us? Had he come by to see how we were? The question gave me no emotion, I thought only that I would like to have someone to talk to.

I looked through the peephole. It was Carrano.

"What do you want?" I asked.

"Nothing. I only wanted to know how you were. I went out early this morning to see my mother and I didn't want to disturb you. But now I'm back, I found a window broken. Has something happened?"

"Yes."

"Can I help you?"

"Yes."

"Can you open the door, please?"

I didn't know if I could, but I didn't tell him. I reached my hand toward the key, I grasped it decisively with my fingers, I moved it slightly, I felt it obedient. The key turned in the lock simply.

"Oh, well," Carrano murmured, looking at me in embarrassment, then he took from behind his back a rose, a single long-stemmed rose, a ridiculous rose offered with a ridiculous gesture by a man not at his ease.

I took it, I thanked him without smiling, I said:

"I have an ugly job for you."

34.

CARRANO WAS KIND. He wrapped Otto in a plastic sheet that he had in the cellar, put him in his car, and, leaving me his cell phone, went to bury him outside the city.

I immediately telephoned the pediatrician and was fortunate, I found him even though it was August. As I was minutely describing to him the child's symptoms, I realized that my pulses were throbbing, so hard that I was afraid the doctor would hear the thud through the cell phone. My heart was swelling again in my breast, it was no longer empty.

I spoke to the doctor at length, making an effort to be precise, and meanwhile I wandered through the house, I tasted the connection between the spaces, touched objects, and at every slight contact with a knickknack, a drawer, the computer, the books, the notebooks, the handle of a door, I repeated to myself: the worst is over.

The pediatrician listened to me in silence, he assured me that there was no reason to worry about Gianni, he said that he would come and see him that evening. Then I took a long cold shower, the needles of water pricked my skin, I felt all the darkness of the months, of the past hours. I saw the rings that I had left upon waking on the edge of the sink and I put on my finger the one with the aquamarine, while, without hesitation, I let the wedding ring fall down the drain. I examined the wound that Ilaria had made with the paper cutter, I put antiseptic on it, covered it with a bandage. I also went, calmly, to separate the dark clothes from the white, I started the washing machine. I wanted the flat certainty of normal days, even though I knew all too well that a frenetic movement upward endured in my body, a darting, as if I had seen an ugly poisonous insect at the bottom of a hole and every part of me were still retreating, my arms and hands waving, feet kicking. I have to relearn—I said to myself—the tranquil pace of those who believe they know where they're going and why.

I concentrated, therefore, on the children, I had to tell them that the dog was dead. I chose my words with care, I tried for the proper tone of fables, but Ilaria wept for a long time anyway and Gianni, although he confined himself at first to a stern look, saying, with a fleeting echo of threatening tones, that Mario had to be informed, immediately afterward went back to complaining of a headache, of nausea.

I was still trying to console them when Carrano returned. I let him in but I treated him coldly, even though he had been so helpful. The children did nothing but call to me from the other room. Convinced as they were that it was he who had poisoned the dog, they didn't want him to set foot in the house, much less have me speak to him.

And I myself had a sensation of repulsion when I smelled on him the odor of dug earth, and to his timidly confidential tone I responded in monosyllables that seemed sporadic drops from a broken faucet.

He tried to tell me about the burial of the dog, but since I didn't show myself interested either in the location of the hole or in the details of the sad task, as he called it, and in fact every so often interrupted him, calling to Gianni and Ilaria, quiet, I'm coming right away, he became embarrassed, and broke off. To cover the children's disruptive cries he began talking about his mother, about the problems of dealing with her old age. He went on until I said that children with long-lived mothers have the misfortune of not really knowing what death is and so never being free of it. He was hurt, he said goodbye with obvious ill humor.

In the course of the day he made no other attempts to see me. I let his rose wither in a vase on my desk, a vase painfully empty of flowers since the long-ago time when, on my birthday, Mario would give me a cattleya, in imitation of Swann. In the evening the flower was already black and bent on its stem. I threw it in the trash.

The pediatrician arrived after dinner, an old man, very thin, very endearing to children because, while he was seeing them, he bowed continually and called them Signor Giovanni, Signorina Illi.

"Signor Giovanni," he said, "show me your tongue immediately."

He examined the boy thoroughly and attributed the illness to a summer virus that caused intestinal upset. It might well be, however, that Gianni had eaten something bad, an egg, for example, or—he said to me later in the living room, in a low voice—that it was a reaction to a powerful sorrow.

As he sat at the desk and prepared to write a prescription, I told him calmly, as if between us there were a habit of confidences of this type, about the breakup with Mario, about that terrible day that was finally about to end, about the death of Otto. He listened to me with attention and patience, he shook his head disapprovingly and prescribed milk enzymes and tenderness for the children, tisane of normality and repose for me. He promised that he would return in a few days.

35.

I SLEPT FOR A LONG TIME, DEEPLY.

Starting the next morning I took good care of Ilaria and Gianni. Since I had the impression that they were watching me closely to see if I was again becoming the mother they had always known or if they had to expect new, sudden transformations, I did my best to reassure them. I read books of fairy tales, I played boring games for hours, I exaggerated the thread of lightheartedness with which I kept at bay the reflux of desperation. Neither of the two, perhaps by a common accord, ever mentioned their father, not even to reiterate that they had to report to him about the death of Otto. I became concerned that they avoided it because they were afraid of wounding me and thus pushing me off course again. I began, then, to bring up Mario, recounting old incidents in which he had been very amusing or had shown himself inventive and clever or had undertaken daredevil acts. I don't know what impression those stories made on them, certainly they listened with absorption, sometimes they smiled in satisfaction. In me they produced only a feeling of annoyance. As I spoke, I noticed that I didn't like having Mario in my memories.

When the pediatrician returned for another visit, he found Gianni in good shape, perfectly healthy.

"Signor Giovanni," he said, "you have a good pink color, are you sure you're not turning into a little pig?"

In the living room, after ascertaining that the children couldn't hear, I asked him, in order to clarify for myself whether I should feel guilty, if Gianni could have been made sick by an insecticide that I had sprayed throughout the house one night for ants. He ruled it out, noting that Ilaria hadn't shown any kind of effects.

"But our dog?" I asked, showing him the can, dented and without the nozzle to spray the poison. He examined it but seemed perplexed, he concluded that he was unable to judge. Finally he returned to the children's room and, with a bow, said goodbye:

"Signorina Illi, Signor Giovanni, it is with true sorrow that I take my leave. I hope that you will soon again be sick, so that I may pay you another visit."

The children were reassured by that tone. For days we continually bowed to each other, saying Signor Giovanni, Signora Mamma, Signorina Illi. Meanwhile, to consolidate a climate of benevolence, I tried to return to normal activities, like a sick person who has been in the hospital for a long time and, partly to overcome the fear of falling ill again, wants to reanchor himself to the life of the healthy. I started cooking again, forcing myself to entice them with new recipes. I began again to slice, brown, salt. I even tried to make sweets, but for sweets I had no vocation, no ability.

36.

I WAS NOT ALWAYS EQUAL to the loving and efficient appearance I wished to have. Certain signs alarmed me. It still happened that I left pots on the stove and didn't even notice the smell of burning. I felt an unfamiliar nausea at the sight of green spots of parsley mixed with the red skins of tomatoes floating on the greasy water of the clogged sink. I was unable to regain the old indifference toward the sticky remains of food that the children left on the tablecloth, on the floor. At times when I was grating cheese the motion became so mechanical, so detached and independent, that the metal cut my nails, the skin of my fingertips. And often I locked myself in the bathroom and—something I had never done—devoted to my body long, detailed, obsessive examinations. I touched my breasts, slid my fingers between the folds of flesh that curled over my belly, I examined my sex in the mirror to see how worn out it was, I checked to see if I was getting a double chin, if there were wrinkles on my upper lip. I was afraid that the effort I had made not to lose myself had aged me. It seemed to me that my hair was thinner, there was more gray, I had to dye it, it felt greasy and I washed it continuously, drying it in a thousand different ways.

But what frightened me above all was the nearly imperceptible images of the mind, the scarce syllables. A thought that I couldn't fix on sufficed, a simple violet flash of meanings, a green hieroglyphic of the brain, for the bad feeling to reappear and panic to mount. Shadows too dense and damp suddenly returned to certain corners of the house, with their noises, the swift movements of their dark masses. Then I caught myself turning the television on and off mechanically, just to have company, or softly singing a lullaby in the dialect of my childhood, or I felt an unbearable anguish because of Otto's empty bowl near the refrigerator, or, suddenly sleepy for no reason, I found myself lying on the sofa caressing my arms, scratching them lightly with the edge of my nails.

On the other hand what helped me greatly, in that period, was the discovery that I was again capable of good manners. The obscene language suddenly disappeared, I no longer felt an urge to use it, I was ashamed of having done so. I retreated to a bookish, studied language, somewhat convoluted, which, however, gave me a sense of security and detachment. I controlled the tone of my voice, anger stayed in the background, the words were no longer charged. As a result, relationships with the external world improved. I managed, with the obstinacy of being nice, to get the telephone fixed, and even discovered that the old cell phone could be repaired. A young clerk in a shop that I miraculously found open showed me how easy it was to put it together, I would have been able to do it even by myself.

To emerge from my isolation, I began right away to make a series of phone calls. I wanted to search out acquaintances who had children the age of Gianni and Ilaria and arrange vacations even of a day or two that would make up for those black months. As I made these calls, I realized that I had a great need to release my hardened flesh in smiles, words, cordial gestures. I got in touch again with Lea Farraco and reacted with nonchalance when she came to see me one day with the cautious air of someone who has something urgent and delicate to discuss. She dragged it out, as was her custom, and I didn't hurry her, showed no anxiety. After making sure that I wouldn't get into a rage, she advised me to be reasonable, she told me that a relationship can end but nothing can deprive a father of his children or children of their father and other things like that. And she concluded:

"You should settle on some days when Mario can see the children."

"Did he send you?" I asked without hostility.

Uneasily she admitted it.

"Tell him that when he wants to see them all he has to do is telephone."

I knew I had to find with Mario the right tone for our future relations, if only for the sake of Gianni and Ilaria, but I had no desire to do it, I would have preferred never to see him again. In the evening after that encounter, before going to sleep, I felt that his smell still emanated from the closets, was exhaled by the drawer of his night table, the walls, the shoe rack. In the past months that olfactory signal had provoked nostalgia, desire, rage. Now I associated it with Otto's death and it no longer moved me. I discovered that it had become like the memory of the odor of an old man who, on a bus, has rubbed off on us the desires of his dying flesh. This fact annoyed me, depressed me. I waited for the man who had been my husband to react to the message I had sent him, but with resignation, not anxiety.

37.

FOR A LONG TIME Otto was my torment. I got furious one afternoon when I caught Gianni, who had put the dog's collar around Ilaria's neck, shouting at her, while she barked, and pulling on the leash: good, down, I'll kick you if you don't stop. I confiscated collar and muzzle, and locked myself in the bathroom, distressed. There, however, with a sudden impulse, as if intending to see how I looked in a late punk ornament, I tried to buckle the collar around my neck. When I realized what I was doing, I began to cry and threw it all in the garbage.

One morning in September, while the children were in the rocky garden, playing and sometimes quarreling with other children, I thought I saw our dog, our own dog, passing quickly by. I was sitting in the shade of a big oak, not far from a fountain in whose constant spray the pigeons slaked their thirst as the drops of water rebounded off their feathers. I was struggling to write about things, and had only a faint perception of the place, I heard the murmur of the fountain, of its cascade among the rocks, among the aquatic plants. Suddenly, out of the corner of my eye, I saw the long, fluid shadow of a German shepherd crossing the lawn. For a few seconds I was certain that it was Otto, returning from the isle of the dead, and thought that again something was crumbling inside me, and was afraid. In reality—I immediately saw—that dog, a stranger, had no real similarity to our unfortunate dog, he wanted only what Otto often wanted after a long run in the park: to drink. He went to the fountain, put the pigeons to flight, barked at the wasps buzzing around the source of the water, and with his purple tongue broke, avidly, the luminous flow. I closed my notebook and watched him, I was moved. He was a stockier, fatter dog than Otto. He seemed less good-natured, but I felt tender toward him just the same. At a whistle from his master he went off without hesitation. The pigeons returned to play under the stream of water.

In the afternoon I looked for the number of the vet, named

Morelli, to whom Mario had taken Otto when necessary. I had never had occasion to meet him, but my husband had spoken of him enthusiastically, he was the brother of a professor at the Polytechnic, a colleague with whom he was friendly. I telephoned the vet, he sounded nice. He had a deep voice, a kind of performing voice, like that of an actor in a movie. He told me to come to the clinic the next day. I left the children with some friends and went.

Morelli's animal clinic was marked by a blue neon sign that was lighted day and night. I descended a long staircase and found myself in a small brightly lit entrance hall with a strong odor, I was greeted by a dark-haired girl who asked me to wait in a side room: the doctor was operating.

In the waiting room were various people, some with dogs, some with cats, even a woman of around thirty with a black rabbit on her lap whom she caressed continuously with a mechanical movement of her hand. I passed the time studying a notice board that displayed offers for breeding purebred animals interspersed with detailed descriptions of lost dogs or cats. From time to time people arrived wanting news of a beloved animal: one asked about a cat recovering from a test, one about a dog who was having chemotherapy, a woman was in anguish over her French poodle who was dying. In that place pain crossed the fragile threshold of the human and expanded into the vast world of domestic animals. I felt slightly dizzy and was covered in a cold sweat when I recognized in the stagnant smell of the place the smell of Otto's suffering, the sum of bad things that it now suggested to me. Soon the feeling that I was responsible for the dog's death was magnified, I felt I had been cruelly careless, my unease increased. Not even the TV in one corner, transmitting the latest harsh news on the deeds of men, could lessen the sense of guilt.

More than an hour passed before I went in. I don't know why, but I had imagined I would find myself facing a fat brute with a bloody shirt, hairy hands, a broad cynical face. Instead I was greeted by a tall man of around forty, dry, with a pleasant face, blue eyes and fair hair over a high forehead, clean in every inch of his body and mind, an impression that doctors know how to give, and he also had the manners of a gentleman who cultivates his melancholy soul while the old world collapses around him.

The doctor listened closely to my description of Otto's agony and death. He interrupted only from time to time to suggest to me the scientific term that to his ear made more reliable my abundant and impressionistic lexicon. Scialorrhea. Dyspnea. Muscular fasciculation. Fecal and urinary incontinence. Epileptoid convulsions and attacks. At the end, he said that it was almost certainly strychnine that had caused Otto's death. He didn't completely rule out the insecticide, on which I kept insisting. But he was skeptical. He uttered obscure terms like diazine and carbaryl, then he shook his head, concluded:

"No, I really would say strychnine."

With him, as with the pediatrician, I felt the impulse to talk about the borderline situation I had been in, I had a strong urge to find the right words for that day. He reassured me, listening without any sign of impatience, looking me in the eye with attention. At the end he said to me soothingly:

"You have no responsibility other than that of being a very sensitive woman."

"Excess of sensitivity can also be a fault," I responded.

"The real fault is Mario's insensitivity," he answered, letting me know by a glance that he could well understand my reasons and considered those of his friend stupid. He also added some gossip on certain opportunistic maneuvers my husband was making to obtain some job or other, things he knew from his brother. I marveled, I didn't know Mario in that aspect. The doctor smiled, showing his very regular teeth, and added:

"Oh, but, apart from that, he's a man with many good qualities."

That last phrase, the elegant jump from malicious gossip to compliment, seemed to me so very successful that I thought of adult normality precisely as an art of that type. I had something to learn.

38.

WHEN I RETURNED HOME that night with the children, I felt the close, comfortable warmth of the apartment for the first time since the abandonment, and I joked with my children until they were persuaded to wash, to go to bed. I had taken off my makeup and was about to go to sleep when I heard a knock at the door. I looked through the peephole, it was Carrano.

I had run into him rarely after he had taken care of burying Otto, and always with the children, always just to say hello. He had his usual air of an unassuming man, shoulders hunched as if he were ashamed of his height. My first impulse was not to open the door, I felt that he could drive me back into bad feelings. But then I noticed that he had combed his hair differently, without a part, his just washed gray hair, and I thought of the care he had taken with his appearance before deciding to climb the flight of stairs and present himself at the door. I also appreciated that he had knocked, in order not to wake the children with the sound of the bell. I turned the key in the lock.

Right away, with a hesitant gesture, he showed me a bottle of cold pinot bianco, he pointed out uneasily that it was the same pinot from Buttrio, of 1998, that I had brought when I went to see him. I told him that on that occasion I had chosen a bottle at random, I didn't mean to indicate any preference. I hated white wine, it gave me a headache.

He shrugged, stood wordless in the hall with the bottle in his hands, it was already streaked with condensation. I took it almost ungraciously, I pointed to the living room, I went to the kitchen to get the corkscrew. When I returned I found him sitting on the sofa, playing with the dented insecticide can.

"The dog really battered it," he commented. "Why don't you throw it away?"

They were innocuous words to fill the silence, yet it bothered me to hear him speak of Otto. I poured him a glass and said:

"Have a glass and go, it's late, I'm tired."

He confined himself to nodding yes awkwardly, but certainly he didn't think I was serious, he expected that slowly I would become more hospitable, more welcoming. I breathed a long sigh of discontent and said:

"Today I went to see a vet, he told me that Otto was poisoned by strychnine."

He shook his head with a sincere expression of sorrow.

"People can be really vicious," he murmured, and for an instant I thought he was alluding, incongruously, to the vet, then I realized that he had in mind those who frequented the park. I looked at him closely.

"What about you? You threatened my husband, you told him you would poison the dog, the children told me."

I saw in his face astonishment and then a genuine distress. I noticed the weary gesture he made in the air as if to distance my words. I heard him murmur, depressed:

"I meant something else, I wasn't understood. I had heard the threat to poison the dog around, I warned you, too…"

But at that point he flared up, took a harsher tone:

"After all, you know perfectly well that your husband thinks he's the master of the world."

It seemed pointless to say that I didn't know it at all. About my husband I had had another idea, and after all he was gone, and with him had gone the meaning that for a long time he had given to my life. It had happened suddenly, as in a movie when suddenly you see a hole opening in a plane at a high altitude. I hadn't had time for even a faint feeling of sympathy.

"He has the flaws of us all," I murmured. "A man like so many others. Sometimes we're good, at times detestable. When I came to you didn't I do shameful things that I never would have dreamed of doing? They were gestures without love, without even desire, pure ferocity. And yet I'm not an especially bad woman."

Carrano seemed to me stricken by those words, alarmed he said:

"I didn't matter to you at all?"

"No."

"And I still don't matter to you now?"

I shook my head, I tried to smile, a smile that would lead him to take the thing as some sort of accident of life, a loss at cards.

He put down the glass, he got up.

"For me that night was very important," he said, "and even more now than then."

"I'm sorry."

He made a half smile, he shook his head no: according to him I felt no sorrow, according to him it was only a way of cutting him off. He murmured:

"You are no different from your husband; after all, you were together a long time."

He went toward the door, I followed him wearily. On the

threshold he handed me the spray can that he had been about to carry away, I took it. I thought he would slam the door when he went out but instead he closed it behind him carefully.

39.

I FRETTED OVER THE OUTCOME of that encounter. I slept badly, I decided to reduce contacts with my neighbor to the minimum, the few things he said had hurt me. When I ran into him on the stairs, I responded to his greeting with an effort and went on. I felt his offended and depressed gaze on my back and wondered how long I would have to endure that vexation of having to retreat from looks charged with pain, mute requests. And yet I deserved it, with him I had been rash.

But things soon took another turn. From day to day, with vigilant care, Carrano himself avoided every encounter. Instead he manifested his presence with signs of devotion from a distance. Now I found in front of my door a shopping bag that, in a hurry, I had left in the lobby, now the newspaper or the pen I had left on a bench in the park. I avoided even thanking him. Yet I continued to revolve in my mind fragments of our conversation and, in thinking about it, discovered that what had disturbed me particularly was the naked accusation that I was like Mario. I couldn't get rid of the impression that he had brought up to me an unpleasant truth, more unpleasant than he himself imagined. I pondered that idea for a long time, especially because, with the reopening of school, and the absence of the children, I found myself with more free time.

I spent the warm mornings of early autumn sitting on a bench in the rocky garden, writing. In appearance they were notes for a possible book, at least that's what I called them. I wanted to cut myself to pieces—I said to myself—I wanted to study myself with precision and cruelty, recount the evil of these terrible months completely. In reality the thoughts revolved around the question that Carrano had suggested to me: was I like Mario? But what did that mean? That we had chosen each other because of affinities and that those affinities had ramified over the years? In what ways did I feel similar to him when I was in love with him? What had I recognized of him in myself, at the beginning of our relationship? How many thoughts, gestures, tones, tastes, sexual habits had he transmitted to me over the years?

In that period I filled pages and pages with questions of this type. Now that Mario had left me, if he no longer loved me, if I in fact no longer loved him, why should I continue to carry in my flesh so many of his attributes? What I had deposited in him had surely been eliminated now by Carla in the secret years of their relationship. But as for me, if all the features that I had assimilated from him had once seemed to me lovable, how, now that they no longer seemed lovable, was I going to tear them out of me? How could I scrape them definitively off of my body, my mind, without finding that I had in the process scraped away myself?

Only at this point—as, during the morning the patches of sun drawn on the lawn among the shadows of the trees slowly shifted, like luminous green clouds in a dark sky—did I return, ashamed, to examine the hostile voice of Carrano. Had Mario really been an aggressive man, certain that he was the master over everything and everyone, and, besides, capable of opportunism, as the vet had suggested? Could the fact that I had never experienced him as a man like that mean that I considered such behavior natural because it resembled mine?

I spent several evenings looking at family photographs. I

searched for signs of my autonomy in the body I had had before meeting my future husband. I compared images of me as a girl with those of later years. I wanted to find out how much my gaze had changed since the time when I began seeing him, I wanted to see if over the years it had ended up resembling his. The seed of his flesh had entered mine, had deformed me, spread me, weighted me, I had been pregnant twice. The formulas were: I had carried in my womb his children; I had given him children. Even if I tried to tell myself that I had given him nothing, that the children were mostly mine, that they had remained within the radius of my body, subject to my care, still I couldn't avoid thinking what aspects of his nature inevitably lay hidden in them. Mario would explode suddenly from inside their bones, now, over the days, over the years, in ways that were more and more visible. How much of him would I be forced to love forever, without even realizing it, simply by virtue of the fact that I loved them? What a complex foamy mixture a couple is. Even if the relationship shatters and ends, it continues to act in secret pathways, it doesn't die, it doesn't want to die.

I took a pair of scissors and, for a whole long silent evening, cut out eyes, ears, legs, noses, hands of mine, of the children, of Mario. I pasted them onto a piece of drawing paper. The result was a single body of monstrous futurist indecipherability, which I immediately threw in the garbage.

40.

WHEN LEA FARRACO reappeared a few days later, I immediately realized that Mario had no intention of dealing directly with me, not even by telephone. The messenger isn't the message, my friend said to me: after that attack on the street, my husband thought that it was better for us to meet as little as possible. But he wanted to see the children, he missed them, he wondered if I would send them to him on the weekend. I said to Lea that I would consult the children and leave the decision up to them. She shook her head, rebuked me:

"Don't do that, Olga, what do you want them to decide."

I didn't pay attention to her, I thought I could handle the question as if we were a trio capable of discussing, confronting, making decisions unanimously or by majority. So as soon as Gianni and Ilaria returned from school, I spoke to them, I said that their father wanted to have them on the weekend, I explained that they should decide whether to go or not, I informed them that they would probably meet their father's new wife (I actually said wife).

Ilaria immediately asked, straight out:

"What do you want us to do?"

Gianni intervened:

"Stupid, she said we're supposed to decide."

They were visibly anxious, they asked if they could consult with each other. They closed themselves in their room and I heard them arguing for a long time. When they came out, Ilaria asked:

"Would you mind if we went?"

Gianni gave her a hard shove and said:

"We've decided to stay with you."

I was ashamed of the test of affection I had tried to make them undergo. Friday afternoon I made them wash carefully, I dressed them in their best clothes, I got two backpacks ready with their things, and brought them to Lea.

On the way they continued to maintain that they had no desire to separate themselves from me, they asked a hundred times how I would spend Saturday and Sunday, finally they got into Lea's car and disappeared with all the intensity of their expectations.

I walked, I went to the movies, I went home, I ate standing up, without setting the table, I watched TV. Lea called me late in the evening, she said the meeting between father and children had been sweet, and touching, she revealed with some unease Mario's actual address, he lived with Carla in Crocetta, in a very nice house that belonged to the girl's family. Finally she invited me to dinner the following night, and although I didn't feel like it, I accepted: the circle of an empty day is brutal, and at night it tightens around your neck like a noose.

I arrived at the Farracos' too early. They tried to entertain me and I forced myself to be cordial. At a certain point I glanced at the set table, mechanically I counted the places, the chairs. There were six. I stiffened: two couples, then me, then a sixth person. I understood that Lea had decided to look after me, she had planned a meeting that might lead to an adventure, a temporary relationship, a permanent arrangement, who knows. Confirmation of this came when the Torreris arrived, a couple I had met at a dinner the year before in the role of Mario's wife, and the vet, Dr. Morelli, whom I had asked about Otto's death. Morelli, who was a good friend of Lea's husband, congenial, up to date on the gossip of the Polytechnic, had clearly been invited to keep me amused.

The whole thing depressed me. This is what awaits me, I thought. Evenings like this. Appearing at the house of strangers, marked as a woman waiting to remake her life. At the mercy of other women who, unhappily married, struggle to propose to me men they consider fascinating. Having to accept the game, not to be able to confess that those men arouse only uneasiness in me, for their explicit goal, known to all present, is to seek contact with my cold body, to warm themselves by warming me, and then to crush me with their role of born seducers, men alone like me, like me frightened by strangers, worn out by failures and by empty years, separated, divorced, widowers, abandoned, betrayed.

I was silent all evening, I slipped an invisible sharp ring around myself, at every remark of the vet's that called for a laugh or a smile I neither laughed nor smiled, once or twice I withdrew my knee from his, I stiffened when he touched my arm and tried to whisper in my ear with unjustified intimacy.

Never again, I thought, never again. Going to the houses of friends who, playing go-between, out of kindness make up occasions for meetings and spy on you to see if things come to a successful conclusion, if he does what he's supposed to do, if you react the way you're supposed to. A spectacle for those already coupled, an entertaining subject when the house is empty and only the remains of the meal are left on the table. I thanked Lea, her husband, and left early, abruptly, when they and their guests were sitting down in the living room to drink and talk.

41.

ON SUNDAY EVENING Lea brought the children home, I felt relieved. They were tired, but it was clear that they were well.

"What did you do?" I asked.

Gianni answered:

"Nothing."

Then it came out that they had been on the merry-go-round, they had gone to Varigotti, to the coast, they had eaten in restaurants for both lunch and dinner. Ilaria spread her arms and said to me:

"I ate an ice cream this big."

"Did you have a good time?" I asked.

"No," said Gianni.

"Yes," said Ilaria.

"Was Carla there?" I said.

"Yes," said Ilaria.

"No," said Gianni.

Before going to bed the little girl asked with some anxiety:

"Are you going to make us go again, next weekend?"

Gianni looked at me from his bed, in apprehension. I answered yes.

In the silent house at night, as I tried to write, it occurred to me that the two children would, over the weeks, between them reinforce the presence of their father. They would better assimilate the gestures, the tones, mixing them with mine. Our dissolved couple would in the two of them be further inflected, intertwined, entangled, continuing to exist when now there was no longer any basis or reason for it. Slowly they will make way for Carla, I thought, I wrote. Ilaria would study her secretly to learn the style of her makeup, her walk, her way of laughing, her choice of colors, and, subtracting and adding, would mix her with my features, my tastes, my gestures whether controlled or careless. Gianni would conceive hidden desires for her, dreaming of her from the depths of the amniotic liquid in which he had swum. Into my children Carla's parents would be introduced, the horde of her forebears would camp with my ancestors, with Mario's. A half-caste din would swell within them. In this reasoning I seemed to capture all the absurdity of the adjective "my," "my children." I stopped writing only when I heard a licking sound, the living shovel of Otto's tongue against the plastic of the bowl. I got up, I went to see if it was empty, dry. The dog had a faithful and vigilant soul. I went to bed and fell asleep.

The next day I began to look for a job. I didn't know how

to do much, but thanks to Mario's transfers I had lived abroad for a long time, I knew at least three languages well. With the help of some friends of Lea's husband I was soon hired by a car-rental agency to take care of international correspondence.

My days became more harried: work, shopping, cooking, cleaning, the children, the wish to start writing again, the list of urgent things to do that I compiled in the evening: get new pots; call the plumber, the sink is leaking; have the blind in the living room fixed; Gianni needs a gym uniform; buy new shoes for Ilaria, her feet have grown.

Now began a continuous frantic rush from Monday to Friday, but without the obsessions of the previous months. I stretched a taut wire that pierced the days and I slid swiftly along it, unthinking, in a false equilibrium with increasing bravura, until I delivered the children to Lea, who in turn delivered them to Mario. Then the void of the weekend opened and I felt as if I were standing, precariously balanced on the rim of a well.

As for the children's return, on Sunday evening, it became a habitual list of complaints. They got used to that oscillation between my house and Mario's and soon stopped being vigilant about what might wound me. Gianni began to praise Carla's cooking, to detest mine. Ilaria told how she took a shower with her father's new wife, she revealed that her breasts were prettier than mine, she marveled at her blond pubic hair, she described her underwear minutely, she made me swear that as soon as her breasts grew I would buy her the same kind of bras, in the same color. Both children took up a new expression that was certainly not mine: they kept saying "practically." Ilaria reproached me because I didn't want to get an expensive cosmetics case that Carla, on the other hand, had made a big show of. One day, during an argument about a jacket that I had bought her and that she didn't like, she cried: "You're mean, Carla is nicer than you."

The moment arrived when I no longer knew if it was better when they were there or when they weren't. For example, I realized that, although they didn't care about hurting me when they talked about Carla, they were jealously watchful to make sure that I devoted myself to them and no one else. Once when they didn't have school, I brought them with me to work. They were unexpectedly well-behaved. When a colleague invited the three of us to lunch, they sat at the table silent, attentive, composed, without quarreling, without exchanging allusive smiles, without throwing around code words, without spilling food on the tablecloth. I later discovered that they had spent the time studying how the man treated me, the attentions he addressed to me, the tone in which I responded, grasping, as children are well able to do, the sexual tension; minimal, a pure lunchtime game, manifested between us.

"Did you notice how he smacked his lips at the end of every sentence?" Gianni asked me with rancorous amusement.

I shook my head, I hadn't noticed it. To illustrate, he smacked his lips comically, making them stick out so that they were big and red, and produced a *plop* every two words. Ilaria laughed until she cried, after every demonstration she said breathlessly: Again. After a little I began to laugh, too, even though their malicious humor disoriented me.

That night Gianni, coming to my room for his usual good night kiss, embraced me suddenly and kissed me on one cheek, going *plop* and spraying me with saliva; then he and his sister went into their room to laugh. And from that moment they both began to criticize everything I did. In tandem they began to praise Carla openly. They made me listen to riddles that she had taught them to prove that I didn't know the answers, they emphasized how comfortable Mario's new house was, while ours was ugly and untidy. Gianni especially soon became unbearable. He shouted for no reason, he broke things, he got into fights with his schoolmates, he hit Ilaria, sometimes he got angry with himself and wanted to bite his own arm, or hand.

One day in November he was coming home from school with his sister, both had bought enormous ice cream cones. I don't know exactly what happened. Maybe Gianni, having finished his cone, insisted that Ilaria give him hers, he was a glutton, always hungry. The fact was that he pushed her so hard that she ended up almost on top of a boy of sixteen, staining his shirt with vanilla and chocolate.

At first the boy seemed to be worried only about the spots, then suddenly he got mad and started fighting with Ilaria. Gianni hit him right in the face with his backpack, bit his hand, and let go his grip only because the other boy began punching him with his free hand.

When I came home from work, I opened the door with the key and heard the voice of Carrano in my house. He was talking to the children in the living room. At first I was rather cold, I didn't understand why he was there in my house, as if he had permission to enter. Then, when I saw the state Gianni was in, with a black eye, his lower lip split, I forgot him and full of anxiety threw myself on the child.

Only slowly did I understand that Carrano, on his way home, had seen my children in trouble, had got Gianni away from the fury of the offended boy, had soothed hysterical Ilaria, and had brought them home. Not only that: he had restored their good mood with stories of punches he had given and received as a boy. The children in fact now pushed me aside and urged him to continue his stories.

I thanked him for that and for all his other kindnesses. He seemed content, his only mistake was yet again to say the wrong thing. He took his leave saying:

"Maybe they're too young to come home alone."

I retorted:

"Young or not, I can't do anything else."

"I could take care of it sometimes," he ventured.

I thanked him again, more coldly. I said that I could manage on my own, and closed the door.

42.

GIANNI AND ILARIA did not improve after that adventure, in fact they continued to make me pay for murky, imagined sins that I had not committed, that were only the black dreams of childhood. Meanwhile, with a twist that was unexpected and difficult to explain, they stopped considering Carrano an enemy—Otto's murderer, they had called him—and, when we met him on the stairs, greeted him with a sort of camaraderie, as if he were a playmate. He tended to respond with rather pathetic winks or restrained gestures of his hand. It was as if he were afraid to be excessive, obviously he didn't want to annoy me, but the children claimed more, they weren't satisfied.

"Hey, Aldo," Gianni would cry, and he wouldn't stop until Carrano decided to murmur, head lowered: Hi, Gianni.

Afterward I grabbed my son and said to him:

"What's all this familiarity? You should be more polite."

But he ignored me, and started making demands like: I want to have my ear pierced, I want to wear an earring, tomorrow I'm dyeing my hair green.

Sundays—when Mario couldn't take them, and that was not infrequently—the hours in the house were filled with irritations, reproaches, scenes. Then I took the children to the park and sent them for infinite rides on the merry-go-round, while autumn blew flocks of red and yellow leaves from the trees, tossing them along the pavement of the streets or dumping them on the water of the Po. But at times, especially when the day was damp and foggy, we went to the city center, and they chased each other around the fountains that sprayed white jets from the pavement while I wandered about idly, holding off the buzz of moving images and crowding voices that at moments of weariness still returned to my head. Sometimes if things felt particularly disturbing, I tried to catch southern accents under the Turinese voices, regaining a fragile, deceptive sense of childhood, an impression of the past, of years accumulated, of a proper distance for memories. More often, I sat apart, on the steps behind the monument to Emanuele Filiberto, while Gianni, armed with a noisy science-fiction gun, a gift from his father, gave his sister harsh lessons on the war of 1915-18, getting excited about the number of soldiers killed, the black faces of the bronze combatants, the guns at their feet. Then, looking toward the flower bed, I stared at three tall mysterious chimneys that rose from the grass and seemed to survey the gray castle like periscopes, I felt that nothing, nothing could console me, even if—I thought—I'm here now, my children are alive and playing with each other, the pain is distilled, it hurt me but didn't break me. With my fingers, sometimes, I touched, above my knee, the scar of the wound that Ilaria had made.

Then something happened that surprised and disturbed me. Right in the middle of the week, at the end of a work day, I found a message from Lea on my cell phone. She invited me to a concert that evening, she said it was really important to her. I listened to her lightly high-pitched voice, with the slight verbosity it assumed when she talked about early music, which she was a great fan of. I didn't feel like going out, but, as with so many things in my life at that time, I forced myself. Then I was afraid she had secretly organized another encounter with the vet, and I hesitated, I had no desire to feel tense all evening. Finally I decided that, vet or not, the concert would relax me, music is always soothing, it loosens the knots of nerves tied tight around the emotions. So I made a lot of telephone calls to find somewhere for Gianni and Ilaria to stay. When I succeeded, I had to convince them that the friends I had decided to entrust them to were not as hateful as they said. They resigned themselves, in the end, even though Ilaria said pointblank:

"Since you're never here, why don't you send us to live with Daddy all the time."

I didn't answer. Every temptation to yell at them was balanced by the terror that I would set off again on some dark pathway, losing myself, so I restrained it. I met Lea, I breathed a sigh of relief, she was alone. We went by taxi to a little theatre outside the city, a sort of nutshell, without corners, smooth. In that setting, Lea knew everyone and was known, and I found myself at my ease, enjoying the reflection of her popularity.

For a while the small room was a hubbub of voices calling and responding, of nods of greeting, a cloud of perfumes and breaths. Then we sat down, the room became silent, the lights dimmed, the musicians entered, the singer.

"They're really good," Lea whispered in my ear.

I said nothing. Incredulous, I had just recognized Carrano among the musicians. In the spotlights he looked different, even taller. He was thin, elegant, every gesture left a bright wake, his hair shone as if it were made of a precious metal.

When he began to play the cello, he lost every remaining trace of the man who lived in my building. He became an exalting hallucination of the mind, a body full of seductive anomalies that seemed to extract from itself impossible sounds, for the instrument was a part of him, alive, born from his chest, his legs, his arms, his hands, from the ecstasy of his eyes, his mouth.

Spurred by the music, I went back, without anxiety, to Carrano's apartment, the bottle of wine on the table, the glasses now full now empty, the dark cloak of that Friday night, the naked male body, the tongue, the sex. I searched in those images of memory, in the man in the bathrobe, in the man of that night, for this other man who was playing, and couldn't find him. How absurd, I thought. I've been to the extreme of intimacy with this skilled and seductive man, but I didn't see it. Seeing him now it seems to me that that intimacy doesn't belong to him, is that of someone who replaced him, perhaps the memory of an adolescent nightmare, perhaps the waking fantasy of a ruined woman. Where am I? Into what world did I sink, into what world did I re-emerge? To what life am I restored? And to what purpose?

"What's wrong?" Lea asked, perhaps worried by my signs of agitation.

I murmured:

"The cellist is my neighbor."

"He's wonderful, do you know him well?"

"No, I don't know him at all."

At the end of the concert the audience applauded and applauded. The musicians left the stage and returned, Carrano's bow was deep and refined, like the curving of a flame pushed by a gust of wind, and his hair of metal fell toward the floor, and then suddenly, when he arched his back and with a forceful motion pulled up his head, returned to order. They played another piece, the beautiful singer moved us with her passionate voice, we applauded again. The audience didn't want to leave, and the musicians, on the wave of applause, were first sucked back into the shadow of the wings, then expelled as if by some rigid command. I was stunned, I had the impression that my skin was binding my muscles and bones too tightly. This was Carrano's true life. Or the false one, which now, however, seemed to me more his than the true one.

I tried to release the euphoric tension I felt, but I couldn't, it seemed to me that the hall had done a headstand, the stage was on the bottom and I was as if high up, looking out from the edge of a hole. Even when one spectator who evidently wanted to go to sleep yelped ironically, and many people laughed, and the applause slowly died away, and the stage emptied, turning a faded green color, and to me it seemed that the shade of Otto had joyously crossed the scene like a dark vein through bright, living flesh, I wasn't frightened. The whole future—I thought—will be that way, life lives together with the damp odor of the land of the dead, attention with inattention, passionate leaps of the heart along with abrupt losses of meaning. But it won't be worse than the past.

In the taxi Lea asked me at length about Carrano. I answered with circumspection. Then, incongruously, as if jealous that I was keeping for myself a man of genius, she began to complain about the quality of his playing.

"He seemed out of shape," she said.

Immediately afterward she added something like: he stayed in the middle of the stream, he was unable to make the leap of quality; a great talent ruined by his own insecurities; an artist diffident through excess of prudence. Just as we reached my house, before saying goodbye, she suddenly started talking about Dr. Morelli. She had brought her cat to him and he had asked insistently about me, if I was well, if I had gotten over the trauma of the separation.

"He told me to tell you," she called to me as I was entering my building, "that he's thought about it some more, he's not sure that Otto's death was caused by strychnine, the facts you gave him weren't sufficient, you need to speak to him again in greater detail."

She laughed maliciously from the window of the taxi, as it started off:

"I feel it's an excuse, Olga. He wants to see you again."

Naturally I never went back to the vet, even though he was

a pleasant man, with a trustworthy air. I was afraid of rash sexual encounters, they repelled me. But above all I no longer wanted to know if it was strychnine or something else that had killed Otto. The dog had fallen through a hole in the net of events. We leave so many of them, lacerations of negligence, when we put together cause and effect. The essential thing was that the string, the weave that now supported me, should hold.

43.

FOR DAYS AFTER THAT EVENING I had to contend with a sharpening of Gianni and Ilaria's complaints. They reproached me for leaving them with strangers, they reproached me for spending time with strangers. Their accusing voices were hard, without affection, without tenderness.

"You didn't put my toothbrush in my bag," Ilaria said.

"I got a cold because they had the radiators turned off," Gianni protested to me.

"They forced me to eat tuna fish and I threw up," the girl whined.

Until the weekend arrived, I was the cause of every misadventure. While Gianni stared at me ironically—did that look belong to me? was that why I hated it? was it Mario's? had he perhaps even copied it from Carla?—practicing grim silences, Ilaria burst into long, piercing cries for no reason, she threw herself on the floor, she bit me, she kicked, taking advantage of small frustrations, a pencil she couldn't find, a comic book with a slightly torn page, her hair was wavy and she wanted it straight, it was my fault because I had wavy hair, her father had nice hair.

I let them go on, I had experienced worse. Besides, it

seemed to me suddenly that ironies, silences, and tantrums were their way, perhaps silently agreed on, for holding off distress and coming up with explanations that might diminish it. I was only afraid that the neighbors would call the police.

One morning we were about to go out, they were late for school, I for work. Ilaria was irritable, unhappy with everything, she was mad at her shoes, the shoes she had been wearing for at least a month and that now suddenly hurt her. In tears she threw herself on the floor of the landing and began kicking the door, which I had just closed. She cried and screamed, she said her feet hurt, she couldn't go to school in that state. I asked her where they hurt, without interest but patiently; Gianni kept repeating, laughing: cut off your feet, make them smaller, so the shoes will fit; I whispered that's enough, come on, quiet, let's go, we're late.

At a certain point there was the click of a lock on the floor below and the voice of Carrano, smudged with sleep, said:

"Can I do anything?"

I flared with shame as if I had been caught doing something disgusting. I put a hand over Ilaria's mouth and held it there forcefully. With the other I energetically made her get up. She was immediately quiet, amazed by my no longer compliant behavior. Gianni stared at me questioningly, I searched for my voice in my throat, a tone that might sound normal.

"No," I said, "thanks, excuse us."

"If there's something…"

"Everything's fine, don't worry, thanks again, for everything."

Gianni tried to cry:

"Hey, Aldo," but I hugged his nose, his mouth hard against my coat.

The door closed discreetly, with regret I noticed that Carrano now intimidated me. Although I knew well all that could come to me from him, I no longer believed what I knew. In my eyes the man on the floor below had become the custodian of a mysterious power that he kept hidden, out of modesty, out of courtesy, out of good manners.

44.

IN THE OFFICE that morning I couldn't concentrate. The cleaning woman must have used an excess of some perfumed cleaning fluid because there was an intense odor of soap and cherries made acidic by the hot radiators. I worked on some German correspondence for hours, but I had no fluency, I was continually consulting the dictionary. Suddenly I heard a male voice coming from the room where clients were received. The voice arrived with perfect clarity, a voice that was coldly acrimonious because certain services, which were costly, had, once the client was abroad, turned out to be inadequate. Yet I heard it from far away, as if it were coming not from a distance of a few feet but from a place in my brain. It was Mario's voice.

I half-opened the door of my room, I looked out. I saw him sitting in front of a desk, in the background a bright-colored poster advertising Barcelona. Carla was with him, sitting beside him, she seemed more graceful, more adult, just slightly plumper, not beautiful. Both appeared to me as if on a television screen, well known actors who were acting out a piece of my life in some soap opera. Mario especially seemed a stranger who by chance had the transient features of a person who had been very familiar to me. He had combed his hair in a way that revealed his broad forehead, framed by thick hair and eyebrows. His face had become thinner, and the prominent lines of the nose, the mouth, the cheekbones formed a design more pleasing than I remembered. He looked ten years younger, the heaviness of his hips, of his chest, of his stomach had disappeared, he even seemed taller.

I felt a sort of light but decisive tap in the middle of my forehead and my hands grew sweaty. But the emotion was surprisingly pleasant, as when a book or a film makes us suffer, not life. I said calmly to the woman behind the desk, who was a friend:

"Is there some trouble?"

Both Carla and Mario turned instantly. Carla leaped to her feet, visibly frightened. Mario stayed seated but he rubbed his nose with thumb and index finger for a few seconds, as he always did when something disturbed him. I said with exaggerated cheerfulness:

"I'm happy to see you."

I moved toward him, and Carla mechanically reached out a hand to pull him close to her, protect him. My husband rose uncertainly, it was clear that he didn't know what to expect. I offered him my hand, we kissed on the cheeks.

"You both seem well," I continued, and shook Carla's hand, too, though she didn't return the clasp, but gave me fingers and palm that felt wet, like meat that has just been defrosted.

"You seem well, too," said Mario, in a tone of perplexity.

"Yes," I answered proudly. "I'm not upset anymore."

"I wanted to call you to talk about the children."

"The number hasn't changed."

"We also have to discuss the separation."

"When you like."

Not knowing what else to say, he stuck his hands nervously in the pockets of his coat and asked in a casual way if anything was new. I answered:

"Not really. The children must have told you: I was sick, Otto died."

"Died?" He was startled.

How mysterious children are. They had been silent about it, perhaps in order not to give displeasure, perhaps in the conviction that nothing that belonged to the old life could interest him.

"Poisoned," I said, and he asked angrily:

"Who did it?"

"You," I said calmly.

"Me?"

"Yes. I discovered that you're a rude man. People respond to rudeness with spite."

He looked at me to see if the friendly atmosphere was about to change, if I intended to start making scenes again. I tried to reassure him, with a tone of detachment:

"Or maybe there was only the need for a scapegoat. And since I wasn't going to be, it was up to Otto."

At that point, in a reflexive gesture, I brushed some scales of dandruff from his jacket, it was a habit of years. He drew back, almost jumped, I said sorry, Carla intervened, to complete with greater care the work that I had immediately suspended.

We said goodbye after he assured me that he would call to make a date.

"If you want you can come, too," I proposed to Carla.

Mario said curtly, without even giving her a glance:

"No."

45.

TWO DAYS LATER he came to the house, loaded with presents. Gianni and Ilaria, contrary to my expectations, greeted him perfunctorily, without enthusiasm, evidently the habit of the weekends had restored to him the normality of father. They immediately started unwrapping the gifts, which pleased them, Mario tried to join in, to play with them, but they didn't want him. Finally he wandered around the room, touching some objects with his fingertips, looking out the window. I asked:

"Would you like some coffee?"

He accepted immediately, followed me into the kitchen. We talked about the children, I told him that, out of the blue, they were going through a difficult time, he assured me that with him they were good, well behaved. At some point he took pen and paper, he laid out a complex schedule of the days when he would have the children, and those when I would, he said that seeing them automatically every weekend was a mistake.

"I hope the money is enough," he said.

"Fine," I said, "you're generous."

"I'll take care of the separation."

I said, to clarify things:

"If I find out that you leave the children with Carla and go off on your own business without paying attention to them, you won't see them anymore."

He looked ill at ease and stared uncertainly at the piece of paper.

"Don't worry, Carla has a lot of good qualities," he said.

"I don't doubt it, but I prefer that Ilaria not learn her childish affectations. And I don't want Gianni to have the desire to put his hands on her chest the way you do."

He abandoned the pen on the table, said despairingly:

"I knew it, nothing is over for you."

I pressed my lips together, hard, then replied:

"Everything is over."

He looked at the ceiling, the floor, I felt that he was dissatisfied. I leaned back in the chair. His chair seemed to have no space for his shoulders, a chair pasted to the kitchen's yellow wall. I realized that on his lips was a mute laugh that I had never seen before. It became him, the expression of a sympathetic man who wishes to show that he knows what's what.

"What do you think of me?" he asked.

"Nothing. Only what I've heard about you surprises me."

"What have you heard?"

"That you're an opportunist and a traitor."

He stopped smiling, he said coldly:

"People who talk like that are no more virtuous than I am."

"I'm not interested in what they are. I only want to know what you are and if you were always like that."

I didn't explain to him that I wanted to eliminate him from my body, get rid of even those aspects of him that, out of a sort of positive bias or out of connivance, I hadn't been able to see. I didn't say to him that I wanted to escape the pull of his voice, of his verbal expressions, of his habits, of his feeling about the world. I wanted to be me. If that formulation even made sense. Or at least I wanted to see what remained of me, once he was removed.

He answered me with feigned melancholy:

"What I am, what I'm not, how do I know."

Wearily he pointed at Otto's bowl that was still sitting in the corner, beside the refrigerator.

"I'd like to get the children another dog."

I shook my head, Otto moved through the house, I heard the light clicking sound of his nails on the floor. I joined my hands and rubbed them slowly against one another, to eradicate the dampness of bad feeling from the palms.

"I'm not capable of replacements."

That night, when Mario left, I read again the pages in which Anna Karenina goes toward her death, leafed through the ones about women destroyed. I read and felt that I was safe, I was no longer like those women, they no longer seemed a whirlpool sucking me in. I realized that I had even buried somewhere the abandoned wife of my Neapolitan childhood, my heart no longer beat in her chest, the veins had broken. The *poverella* had become again an old photograph, the petrified past, without blood.

46.

THE CHILDREN, too, suddenly began to change. Although they were still hostile toward each other, ready to come to blows, they slowly stopped getting mad at me.

"Daddy wanted to get us another dog, but Carla didn't want to," Gianni said to me one night.

"You'll get one someday when you live on your own," I consoled him.

"Did you love Otto?" he asked.

"No," I answered, "while he was alive, no."

I was astonished by the frankness and composure with which I now managed to answer all the questions they asked. Will Daddy and Carla make another child? Will Carla leave Daddy and find someone younger? Do you know, when she's using the bidet he comes in and pees? I argued, I explained, sometimes I even managed to laugh.

Soon I got in the habit of seeing Mario, telephoning him about daily problems, protesting if he was late in putting money in my account. At some point I noticed that his body was changing again. He was getting gray, his cheekbones were swelling, his hips, his stomach, his chest were getting heavy again. Sometimes he tried growing a mustache, sometimes he left his beard long, sometimes he shaved completely with great care.

One evening he appeared at the house without warning, he seemed depressed, he wanted to talk.

"I have something unpleasant to tell you," he said.

"Tell me."

"I can't stand Gianni, Ilaria gets on my nerves."

"It's happened to me, too."

"I only feel good when I'm not around them."

"Yes, sometimes it's like that."

"My relationship with Carla will be ruined if we continue to see them so often."

"Could be."

"Are you well?"

"Me, yes."

"Is it true that you don't love me anymore?"

"Yes."

"Why? Because I lied to you? Because I left you? Because I humiliated you?"

"No. Just when I felt deceived, abandoned, humiliated, I loved you very much, I wanted you more than in any other moment of our life together."

"And then?"

"I don't love you anymore because, to justify yourself, you said that you had fallen into a void, an absence of sense, and it wasn't true."

"It was."

"No. Now I know what an absence of sense is and what happens if you manage to get back to the surface from it. You, you don't know. At most you glanced down, you got frightened, and you plugged up the hole with Carla's body."

He made a grimace of annoyance, he said to me:

"You have to have the children more. Carla is exhausted, she has exams to take, she can't take care of them, you're their mother."

I looked at him attentively. It was really true, there was no longer anything about him that could interest me. He wasn't even a fragment of the past, he was only a stain, like the print of a hand left years ago on a wall.

47.

THREE DAYS LATER, returning home from work, I found on the doormat, on a piece of paper towel, a tiny object that I had trouble identifying. It was a new gift from Carrano, by now I was used to these silent kindnesses: recently he had left me a button I had lost, also a hair clip I was very attached to. I realized that this was a conclusive gift. It was the white nozzle of a spray can.

I sat down in the living room, the house felt empty, as if it had never been inhabited by anyone but puppets of papier-maché or by clothes that had never hugged living bodies. Then I got up, I went to look in the storage closet for the spray can that Otto had played with the night before that terrible day in August. I looked for the marks of his teeth, I ran my fingers over it to feel the dents. I tried to stick the cap onto the can. When it seemed to me that I had succeeded, I pressed with my index finger but there was no spray, only a slight odor of insecticide.

The children were with Mario and Carla, they would return in two days. I took a shower, carefully made up my face, put on a dress that I knew looked nice and went to knock on Carrano's door.

I felt myself observed through the peephole for a long time: I imagined that he was trying to calm the pounding of his heart, that he wanted to remove from his face the emotion inspired by that unexpected visit. Existence is this, I thought, a start of joy, a stab of pain, an intense pleasure, veins that pulse under the skin, there is no other truth to tell. To make the emotion even stronger I rang the bell again.

Carrano opened the door, his hair was disheveled, his clothes were in disarray, the belt of his pants undone. He smoothed the dark fabric with both hands, adjusting it so as to cover the belt. Seeing him, I had a hard time realizing that he knew how to produce warm sweet notes, to give the pleasure of harmony.

I asked him about his last gift, I thanked him for the others. He was evasive, he was brief, he said only that he had found the spray top in the trunk of his car and had thought that it would be helpful to me in putting order into my feelings.

"It must have been in Otto's paws or his fur or even in his mouth," he said.

I thought with gratitude that in those months, discreetly, he had worked to sew up around me a world that could be trusted. He had now arrived at his kindest act. He wanted me to understand that I no longer had to be frightened, that every movement could be narrated with all its reasons good and bad, that, in short, it was time to return to the solidity of the links that bind together spaces and times. With that gift he was trying to exonerate himself, he was exonerating me, he was attributing the death of Otto to the chance of the games of a dog at night.

I decided to go along with him. Because of his constitutional wavering between the figure of the sad colorless man and that of the virtuoso creator of luminous sounds, capable of making your heart swell and giving you an impression of intense life, he seemed to me at that moment the person I needed. I doubted of course that that spray top was really from my insecticide, that he had really found it in the trunk of his car. Yet the intention with which he offered it to me made me feel light, an attractive shadow behind frosted glass.

I smiled at him, I brought my lips to his, I kissed him.

"Has it been very bad?" he asked me in embarrassment.

"Yes."

"What happened to you that night?"

"I had an excessive reaction that pierced the surface of things."

"And then?"

"I fell."

"And where did you end up?"

"Nowhere. There was no depth, there was no precipice. There was nothing."

He embraced me, he held me close to him for a while, without saying a word. He was trying to communicate silently that, through his mysterious gift, he knew how to make meaning stronger, to invent a feeling of fullness and joy. I pretended to believe him and so we loved each other for a long time, in the days and months to come, quietly.

Elena Ferrante was born in Naples, Italy. Though one of Italy's most important and acclaimed contemporary authors, she has shunned public attention and willfully kept her identity a mystery. *The Days of Abandonment* is Elena Ferrante's second novel. She is also the author of *Troublesome Love* (*L'amore molesto*), to be published by Europa Editions in 2006.